I COME AS A THIEF

"... a tautly written, fast paced, and above all believable examination of the religious foundation of our public code of ethics. At a time when these ethics seem to have about as much chance of surviving as the virtue of a maiden in a Third Avenue singles bar, it is bracing to see an intelligent novelist who knows his craft still making a valid, dramatic case for them."

Life

"One of Louis Auchincloss's very best ... His eye on the New York scrabbling scene has never been sharper, more stringent and telling."

Stephen Birmingham

"This story of Mr. Auchincloss's is different and I like it: it is a novel of principle, which is rare in any season."

The Atlantic

Mr. Auchincloss spins a suspenseful series of developments, full of unexpected turns and subtle moral implications ... the novel comes out impressively, disturbingly, provocatively."

The Wall Street Journal

"Intriguing, never for a moment dull ... an elegant read."

Cleveland Plain Dealer

Also by Louis Auchincloss

THE HOUSE OF FIVE TALENTS
A LAW FOR THE LION
POWERS OF ATTORNEY
PURSUIT OF THE PRODIGAL
VENUS IN SPARTA
SYBIL

LOUIS AUCHINCLOSS

I COME AS A THIEF

AVON
PUBLISHERS OF BARD, CAMELOT, DISCUS, EQUINOX AND FLARE BOOKS

AVON BOOKS
A division of
The Hearst Corporation
959 Eighth Avenue
New York, New York 10019

Published by arrangement with Houghton Mifflin Company.
Library of Congress Catalog Card Number: 77-190053.

First Avon Printing, July, 1973.

Printed in the U.S.A.

For my good friend
and faithful correspondent

George T. Keating

with deep gratitude
for all his advice and encouragement
in my work

Behold, I come as a thief. Blessed is he that watcheth, and keepeth his garments, lest he walk naked, and they see his shame.

—Revelation, XVI, 15

Part I

1

Lee Lowder had hoped, after Tony's defeat in the State Senate election, that their life might be given back to them. After all, he had not been a regular politician and had accepted the nomination only because the Democrats had desperately needed a standard bearer to wage the hopeless if important fight in the Lowders' traditionally Republican Manhattan district. And Tony had done better than anyone had dared to predict. He had dragged his much older and bitterly conservative opponent from the confident back rooms of right wing politics to the sound truck and the television debate; he had attracted statewide notice; he had rolled up the Democratic vote from its usual 25 percent to a figure so close to 50 that a recount had been necessary. Ex-Governor Horton had come to see Lee to assure her that there would now be a period of rest and reflection.

"We have great ideas for Tony in the party, Lee, but I want to be sure he makes no false steps. He may be only forty-three, but that's no chicken for a man who's just lost his first race. We must use him carefully. The President owes us a Democrat on the Securities and Exchange Commission when Tom Surtees retires this spring. This may be a long shot, but I have a hunch I might swing it for Tony. So I'm going to suggest he use the interim to learn the ropes as Special Assistant to the Regional Director here in New York."

Lee had contemplated the sharp, pink eyes in that wide, white, doughy face. "And what would the Securities and Exchange Commission lead to?"

"Anything at all. Attorney General of the state. Who knows? Perhaps Congress."

"But he would have a minute to catch up on his family?"

"Oh, yes. These special assistant jobs . . ." Horton shrugged. "You know, they're what you make them. Call it a two-month vacation if you like."

"But Tony makes so much of everything!"

"Poor Lee. You hate politics, don't you?"

"Oh, no! I like it!"

It had been true—at times. There had been excitement, exhilaration in the campaign. To see Tony's earnest, square jaw, his small, inquisitive, smiling eyes, his curly gray hair on billboard after billboard, looming over words that demanded all kinds of wonderful but perfectly practical things, to hear his deep resonant voice on radio and television denouncing the slick, tricky slogans of the extreme right, to hear the roars with which he was greeted at rallies, well, it almost convinced one for the moment that something *could*—or even would—be done. And then had she not come of a family that had been just the opposite, that had never adventured beyond the strictly private life, that had sniggered over the egotistical motives which they had imputed to the smallest self-exposure, whether in amateur theatricals or running for public office? It was thrilling to feel your family trounced.

"I suppose the trouble with all of us," she mused, "is that we're so sure that our sense of proportion is right. Too much or too little is always what other people are guilty of. That's why I absolutely know that Mummie and Daddy are stick-in-the-muds and Tony isn't enough of one. But Lee Lowder? Oh, she's perfect, of course! The way she divides her time between friends and children, between social life and home life, is just exactly right. How could it not be?"

"How old are the children now, Lee?"

"Isabel is fourteen and Eric twelve. Both still at home and at private day schools. Everything still perfect. Pre-hair and pre-pot. But I know what we're on the threshold of. That's why I need Tony more at home right now."

Well, Tony had taken the Governor's offered job, and, as Horton had predicted, he had found it much less demanding than his law practice, but this had done Lee little good, for he seemed to have as many meetings as ever. What could you do with a man whose curiosity and interest were so easily and constantly re-aroused? Where was he now, at six o'clock, on a dull winter's evening, while she sat with Eric in the living room, she with her bills, he with his homework, reluctant audience to Isabel's heavy pounding of the "Marche Militaire" on the upright piano in the dining alcove? At the Turtle Bay Settlement House? At the Boys'

Club? At the Young Democratic Club? At Joan Conway's? She frowned. At his mother's? Oh, no, *she* was coming there (how could Lee forget?) for a drink—or, as Mrs. Lowder always put it, for "a spot of sherry."

"What are you studying?" she asked Eric, to help thrust off this chronic irritation.

Eric looked up at her with his clear gaze of unexpressed impatience. He was thin, painfully thin, with a long, craggy, spotty face and an odd row of yellow bangs. If she could only transfer to him some of Isabel's flesh! "Pope Paul the third and the Counter Reformation."

"Doesn't your class feel that's irrelevant?"

"To what?"

"Oh, to all that's going on in the world today."

"If you were strapped to a steel chair, after having both legs broken on the wheel, and then lowered over a slow fire, you might not have found the Counter Reformation so irrelevant."

"My God, is *that* what you're reading about?"

Eric shrugged, with a meager smile, and resumed his reading. Lee wondered if he might be the herald of a reaction in youth. He was such a solitary child, with such high marks and so few friends.

"Isabel!" she called. "Must you pound so?"

"Miss Downey says I should play it with feeling."

There were moments when Lee was almost appalled at how little she and Tony had to show for their lives. He had been earning forty thousand a year before he had taken the government job, but it had all gone in taxes, rent and tuition. Everything they had in the world was contained in this Lexington Avenue flat, with its living room, dining alcove, foyer, two master bedrooms and maid's room (for Eric). And what a miscellany it was. Tony would never part with family things. Who else in the world would have kept the ugly amateur portrait of his contractor grandfather with muttonchop whiskers, the two atrocious Hudson River School landscapes, the horsehair sofa, the big black walnut breakfront with the sets of Cooper and Louisa May Alcott? Small wonder that her own father did not care to part with his few treasured "old New York" items to such a son-in-law. And yet, in spite of everything, she loved it all. She even loved to walk down the dull brown characterless corridor from the elevator past the closed anonymous doors, anticipating the one that would open upon the crowded, glowing warmth of her own home.

"Isabel, please! Or I'll tell Miss Downey to give you nothing but Debussy."

Yet what did she have if one took away Tony? What could she show for the thirty-eight years of her life? Oh, Eric and Isabel, of course. That went without saying—or did it? But there was nothing, so to speak, "star-like" about herself as a mother or housewife, as a friend or daughter, or even as a dabbler in social work (all Tony's causes). No, the everything about Lee Lowder had to be her love for Tony, as she faced again and again—probably too much. He represented the near total of her emotional capital.

The front doorbell rang loudly. Had he lost his key? Oh, no, how could she forget again—Mrs. Lowder! Lee hurried out to admit her mother-in-law, dreading the moment as she opened the door when a scrim would descend over the apartment, over her whole life, like the scrim in *Das Rheingold* that shows the gods as old when Freia is taken by the giants. Instantly she would see her things as Mrs. Lowder saw them.

"You look surprised, my dear. Weren't you expecting me?"

"Of course. Come in."

Isabel might have been hitting the keys with a kitchen pounder, but she was still not loud enough to muffle the sound of Eric urinating in the bathroom off the hall corridor.

"Eric, I've told you a hundred times to close that door! One of these days I'm going to roast *you* over a slow fire."

"Lee, what a dreadful idea to put in the child's mind! Don't scare him!"

"Eric's mind is more full of horrors than Fox's *Book of Martyrs*. My pigmy imagination could never hope to add to it."

In the living room Dorothy Lowder sat in the smallest, stiffest chair as if it were the only one that she could trust not to buckle. She gave the impression of being swathed and scarved, like a pre-World War I automobilist. Her eyes were big and blue, round and unhappy, anticipating the hurt which they elicited. But if her frizzed gray hair and round face suggested an Irish Clara Bow, kissed by time, her dumpy, mauve-draped figure evoked the contrast of a vamp, a Theda Bara who had succumbed to sweet cakes.

"I wonder if Tony doesn't have something on his mind. He seems so tired these days."

"I guess he worries about his father."

"Oh, I can't think it's just that."

But Lee was determined to keep the ball of

reproach in Mr. Lowder's court. "He hates to see his father's memory going. And getting in to see Mr. Lowder so often, all the way across the park, isn't the easiest thing in the world."

"Well, of course, he's a wonderful son. Nobody knows that better than I. For all the help I get from Susan and Philip! I can't understand their attitude. In my day a family was a family. It was a case of mutual obligations . . ."

And Mrs. Lowder was off on the Dalys. Eric and Isabel retreated to their rooms. They knew all about the fortune which Grandpa Daly had made and lost, except for the poor remnant on which Mrs. Lowder still lived. They knew about the five handsome Daly sons, the five pretty Daly daughters, the big white shingled house in Larchmont, the hospitality, the cheer, the warmth of it all. There were still moments when Lee could feel sorry for her mother-in-law, trapped in a dry old age with a smiling booby of a husband, but didn't she have Tony? A good part of him, anyway?

"My sister Vinnie still has all that," Mrs. Lowder complained. "She has thirty-two descendants, and there's never a day in the calendar that one of them doesn't come in to see her. Perhaps my trouble was in giving up the Church. There's something so dry and dead about Episcopalianism."

"But, Mrs. Lowder, you have three perfectly good children!"

"And only one of them married. What good is Susan to me, I'd like to know? When old maids stayed at home with the old folks, at least they had that use. Susan's so busy at Legal Aid, she can hardly get in to see us on weekends."

"Susan is a very useful woman."

"Not to those that bred her, she isn't. And Philip, what does he care about his parents? What does he care about but that horrid young man he lives with? Ugh. I can hardly hold my head up when I think about it."

"You should try to understand that, Mrs. Lowder. Parents are learning to accept homosexuality today."

"Please don't use that word!" Mrs. Lowder gesticulated violently, as if she were thrusting off some assaulting creature. "Can you imagine what they *do* to each other? Even to think of it is too repulsive."

"I know what they do. Would you like me to tell you?"

"Never. My dear Lee, you're sometimes appallingly modern."

"But you should *love* Philip and Susan. It's so awful, this American habit of thinking people have no lives unless they marry and breed. As if we were hamsters."

"Lee! You sometimes go too far. How can you, a mother, think I would not love my own children?"

"Oh, anybody can *not* love somebody else," Lee retorted, weary of it. "Anyway, you have Tony."

"Oh, yes, we all have Tony."

And there he was, standing in the foyer, taking off his raincoat. What did he do to a room? Was it his build? His bigness? His large, square, generous face? Or was it the contagious friendliness of those intent, attentive gray eyes? Or the easy impassivity of his manner and the strange fearlessness that radiated from him? Or was she simply a romantic fool? Plenty of people, she knew, did not think Tony was in the least extraordinary. Indeed, her own father found him rather ordinary. And what for that matter had he really accomplished in his life but practice law with a very moderate success and lose a campaign for the State Senate? But this was heresy.

"Darling!" She hurried out to the foyer to fling her arms around his neck.

"Hey, what's up? Did you hear I was dead or something? How are you, Ma?"

Mrs. Lowder's answer was lost in the noisy return of the children who did not scruple to throw in their grandmother's face that the excuse of homework for their retirement had been a sham. Isabel, whose broad face seemed broader framed by straight blonde hair, demanded that her father settle an argument with Eric that had raged, except for school, since breakfast.

"Eric says that welfare shouldn't pay a mother for more than one illegitamate child!"

"It just encourages them to have more," Eric retorted.

"And they don't take proper care of them. Everyone knows that. They let them run around the streets and look for heroin and grow up to be criminals and mug us. *Us*, who pay for their welfare!"

"I must say, I think it's extraordinary what children discuss these days," Dorothy Lowder interposed. "I really wonder what good it will do Isabel or Eric to know about such things at their ages. Still, I can't help agreeing with Eric."

"But Grandma! It's a woman's natural function to have a baby."

"In a civilized world, Isabel, we must learn to control our natural functions."

"Oh, I'm for birth control, of course."

"That's not what I was trying to say at all. I was trying to say . . ."

"But birth control isn't the point," Isabel interrupted. "A civilized government should be responsible for every child born under it."

"The government can still be responsible," Eric pointed out. "But not by paying the mother welfare. It should take the child away from her and bring it up properly."

"Take the child away from its own mother!"

"Why not? If she's obviously unfit? The way half of them are."

Lee could see that Tony, looking from one to the other, was debating, not how he should decide, but how he should phrase his decision. Isabel, of course, had to win—she knew that—but she could not altogether repress an impulse of sympathy for Eric. He was so serious, so industrious, so conscientious, and Isabel was such a . . . well, such a mess. Eric made her think of some hard-working settler in the wilderness who finds the small patch that he has staked out and cultivated threatened by indolent Indians.

"Eric," Tony said gravely. "Every child, however born, is a human being, with as much right to grow up as you have."

"I know that, Dad."

"Of course, you know it. It's nothing to know it. You have to feel it."

"Why? Why do I have to?"

"Because to the extent that you fail to feel it, you fail to be alive."

Eric put on his look of "So it's going to be one of *those* evenings" and left the room. Isabel returned to her piano. Dorothy Lowder drew her round face into a longer shape, as if she were trying to remold it with thoughts of dignity and sadness.

"I was just telling Lee how tired you look. Is it the new job?"

"Oh, no, the job's easy enough. All I do is check the financial houses to see their capital's up to snuff. It's my own capital that worries me. This market's a ghastly headache."

"Tony! You don't mean you've been speculating."

Tony looked as if this were the last thing he needed after a long day. "I've been trying to make some money, Ma. And it's not easy in a recession."

"But you should have learned from your grandfather's example. Speculation was always the ruin of the Dalys."

Tony winked at Lee. "I guess it's my sad destiny to offer another proof of that."

"Why do you have to stay in government if it pays so badly?" his mother persisted. "Why can't you go back to your law firm?"

Lee intervened indignantly. "Because if Tony's ever to get anywhere in politics it has to be now."

"Why does Tony have to 'get anywhere' in politics? Is politics the end of the world? Personally, I've never really seen Tony as a professional politician."

"Why, he's a natural politician, Mrs. Lowder. Everyone who saw him in the campaign recognized that."

"Oh, I don't say he doesn't do it well, Lee. Of course, he does. Tony does everything well."

"I thought you were just suggesting that he has no talent for speculating."

"Well, that's hardly a great art, is it?"

"It had better be, I guess, if it's what he's doing!"

"You take one up so fast on things, Lee. I simply meant that Tony may be too nice for politics."

"Too nice or too soft?"

"Too *nice*, Lee. I shan't have words put in my mouth. Politicians—successful ones, that is—have to be hard-boiled. Tony would always be worrying about some lame duck. That's why I think he'll do better in his profession. There his lame ducks can pay."

"I never heard anything so cynical," Lee retorted. She was beginning to be uncomfortable at the prospect of really losing her temper. "Why can't you admit, Mrs. Lowder, that the only reason you don't want Tony in politics is that you don't want him to go to Washington and leave you?"

"Now, darling . . ." Tony was beginning, but his mother, quite as angry now as Lee, cut him off.

"Well, is it so unnatural for a mother to lean on her own son?" Then, after a moment's silence in which they all showed the shock of how far they had gone, Dorothy took a loftier tone. "Don't worry, Lee, it's not going to last forever. One of these days you and Tony will be perfectly free to go to Washington or anywhere else you please. And there may be a bit of money for you, too. Not much, I fear, but a bit."

"But Tony can't wait, Mrs. Lowder. If he's going to do anything, he's got to do it now."

"I wasn't suggesting that he would have to wait for long."

"Oh, in these days people live forever."

Mrs. Lowder rose with the dignity of an old print of Sarah Siddons playing Queen Katharine at her trial. "Let us hope for some exceptions to that unfortunate rule. Perhaps, Tony, you won't mind helping me to get a taxi."

When they had gone, Lee saw Isabel in the dining alcove. She had come back to practice and had heard it all.

"If you're ever fool enough to marry a man with a mother, Isabel Lowder," Lee exclaimed fiercely, "never give her an exit line like that."

2

What humiliated Lee about the complaint that she inwardly nursed against Tony was that it was the commonest complaint on the American domestic scene: that he did not belong to her as much as she wanted and had not, since their honeymoon. He had not, she was fairly sure, belonged to anyone else—he did not, for example, belong to Joan Conway or even to his mother—but that did not prevent her feeling a lack, over and above (or at least so she fancied) the lack that every human being who loves another human being is doomed to feel in the bottom of that other's response.

"I know it doesn't do any good, because nobody ever listens to anyone else," her own mother had retorted on the only occasion when Lee had confided in her about this. "But I must still tell you that you're a perfect little idiot. Tony is doing very well as a husband and father, and he's certainly a good son-in-law. Always so polite and interested. I never feel it's perfunctory, though I suppose it must be."

"But it's not perfunctory!" Lee protested. "It never is with Tony. That's just what I mean. He's devoted to you. Sometimes I think he's devoted to everybody."

"Thanks."

"Well, I even think he's devoted to me."

"Then what on earth are you complaining about?"

"That he loves us all just the same amount."

"Really, Lee, you're too ridiculous. Anyway, I can't imagine why people think parents have any influence. You've always been wildly romantic, and I don't think anyone ever accused your father or me of that. But you might do well to borrow a leaf out of our unromantic notebook: 'Let well enough alone.' If I kept picking away at your father the way you pick at Tony, I might find out that he was less amiable than I suppose. Human beings aren't such great shakes, my dear. We all wear masks, for decency's sake. This modern business of yanking them off can be very foolish."

Perhaps Lee would not have been so troubled if Tony, throughout their brief courtship and honeymoon, had not lived so incredibly up to her ideal. She had originally been quite humble about her ideals—accepting her mother's conservative tradition—until he had seemed, by his dazzling conduct, to be saying: "No, it's all right; your dreams were not presumptuous; a husband, a lover, *can* be all that." It was really a pity to be capable of playing a role to such perfection if he could not maintain it. Or was it better to have one perfect memory than none at all?

"He looks lucky to me," her hostess had said at the cocktail party in the stuffy little garden behind the converted brownstone where Lee had first met him. "He looks like the kind of man who can always get a taxi on a rainy day."

Or a girl. Or a pretty girl. One who was twenty-three and thought that life was over because a short story had been rejected by *The New Yorker*. He had looked, at twenty-seven, much as he still did: tall, with those broad shoulders and a face that managed to be at once square and sensitive, and he moved with the awkward heaviness of some natural athletes, exuding, perhaps simply through his frequent deep laughs, an air of gaiety oddly inconsistent with an appearance that seemed more adapted to sobriety, even to puritanism. Lee had not known in the least what to make of him. His sympathy about the short story was extraordinary. He did not seem to be putting it on, which was quite as much as could have been expected of any bachelor lawyer who wanted a date, and a late one, for the evening. No, it was more as if the rejected short story had been his own disappointment. His attitude had cured her of literary ambition forever, but it had given her something else to cope with.

Everyone had always been on his side from the beginning. Any hope that her father might be shocked by the fact that his family lived west of Central Park, that his maternal grandfather had been an Irish immigrant and his paternal one at least partly Jewish, that he had not gone to an acceptable preparatory school or an Ivy League college, was soon dispelled. "Nobody cares about that sort of thing any more," Mr. Bogardus had snapped at her. "Tony's a natural gentleman. Besides, he got a silver star in Korea." Lee was to be denied the romance of rejection. Could it be that her parents were afraid she would get nobody?

And then the honeymoon in Bermuda. If she had written about it as she saw it in her own mind, she could not have sold it to *True Romance*, let alone *The New Yorker*. It would have been deemed far too sentimental, too gooey. She had been frightened at moments, wondering if it was quite safe to take one's foot off the earth and place it in a third-rate movie. Tony was so considerate, so masterful, so entertaining, so funny. Might she have been relieved to notice, when he studied the menu, ordered the wines, demonstrated his competence in such matters, that he was just the tiniest bit common? But he wasn't.

Only his own father, vacant, foolish, perpetually smiling Mr. Lowder, seemed to doubt him. "Tony's a fine fellow," he told her, "but he doesn't seem to be getting anywhere. Maybe he's too nice."

Was that it? Fifteen years later she still didn't know. There was a privacy in Tony that never yielded to any assault, that never showed a dent. If he rarely displayed irritability and hardly ever bad temper, he was still ineluctable in his determinations. He seemed to be always busy: in his law practice, in his boys' club and settlement house, with the myriad personal problems of his vast number of not very attractive friends. He never earned enough money, for he was a very free spender, and encouraged her to be the same. Yet they always seemed just to manage. He would leave the apartment at night to meet someone who telephoned without explaining why. "Ed's in a jam. I've got to go," was all that he would say. He took hold of her life, encouraged her to be an active citizen, to go on the Junior Committee of the Turtle Bay Settlement House. "You must make something of yourself," he would emphasize.

Why? For years she had not been able to make out if he had a purpose. He had left a big downtown law firm to form a small midtown partnership which had done moderately well but not very much more than that. He had made a name for himself in boys' welfare and recreation, but so had others. He was popular with many friends, but so were others. And then, suddenly, had come his nomination for the State Senate, and, for six months, everything at last had seemed to jell. Volunteers had flocked to his headquarters; money had filled the mail. Tony, like a squirrel long watching a high bird feeder, had finally leaped and landed securely at the first try. There had even been a wild columnist in *The Village Voice* who had entered his name in the list of future presidential aspirants. The whole thing had been a dazzling experience and had made her wonder if all that had mystified her in Tony was not simply that he was a public man.

"I've made a great decision!" she exclaimed, as soon as the front door opened and he had returned, after taking his mother down. "I've decided that I really want you to be a politician. And not just to irritate your mother, either."

"You're trying to get out of the scolding you know you deserve. Talk about wet hens! I had to sit in the lobby half an hour calming Mother down."

"Oh, she loved it. You know she loved it. So did I. I want to be taken out to dinner to celebrate my great decision."

"We're bust."

"I have some cash."

At the Italian restaurant two blocks south, in a back booth, Lee sipped her drink and felt strangely elated. Was it happiness?

"Will you excuse me to make a call to Max?"

Her elation collapsed. "Oh, Tony, you're *always* calling Max. I thought now you were out of the law you could leave your partners alone for a bit."

"But, darling, I'm in so many things with Max."

"What things?" She detested Max Leonard. She had always detested him. She was convinced that he had done Tony a disfavor in persuading him to leave Hale & Cartwright to set up on their own. Max had had no future in the bigger firm; Tony might have had. And Max was so relentlessly charming, so pallidly handsome, so busy-busy, so scheming. She thought he loved Tony more than he loved his snobby little wife. She thought he was in love with Tony. "I hate Max."

"You've never given Max his due. He's been a very good friend. It was he, after all, who got me into politics."

"What things are you in with him?" she repeated.

"Business things. I've told you, but you never listen. Max and I have gone into a joint capital venture. It's backing a small restaurant chain in Jersey. And then there's the stock in that new computer firm, Herron . . ."

"Why?" she interrupted.

"Why a computer firm?"

"No. Why do you have to go into these things?"

"To make money, of course."

"Why do you need so much money? I thought you only wanted to add to your income a bit."

"All right, Lee. Let's talk about something else."

Gin always made her irritable, and she knew that she had to get hold of herself. "No, I'm interested," she said. "Really interested. Why do we have to be rich?"

"Please, Lee. Tell me about your day. Did you go to the Boys' Club?"

"No, I want to talk about why you want to be rich. Aren't I and the children enough for you?"

"Oh, Lee."

"I'm not being soppy. I want to know. You never tell me what you're really thinking. Please do. Just once." She saw that she was only antagonizing him, and she paused again to drain some of the emotion out of her tone. "I'd like to know the role of wealth in our future. Seriously. Maybe you're right. Maybe we *ought* to be wealthy."

Tony looked at her with contained exasperation. "Well, it's not fashionable in liberal circles to admit the importance of money in politics, but all the same, there it is. If you're a poor Republican, you can get your money from business. But it's not so simple for poor Democrats. The big ones have all been rich: Roosevelt, Stevenson, Kennedy, Johnson, Harriman . . ."

"You mean they have to have money for campaigns?"

"They have to have it for the whole way of life. How do you live when you're out of office? How do you live—for that matter—when you're *in*? A man with half a million bucks behind him isn't so nervous about next November. And besides, people trust him more. In an affluent society—and, God, is it affluent!—the politician must have something, too. The English always understood this. Disraeli had to marry a rich widow before going into politics . . ."

"It's a pity you didn't think of that before you married me."

"There are other ways of making money, you know."

"Like Max."

"Well, Max is part of it, sure."

"And how are they doing, your things?"

"Not well at all!" he exclaimed with a cheerful laugh. "Which reminds me. I've got to make that call."

Alone, Lee drank another Martini and tried to consider her mortification more calmly. Max always prevailed over her, but then didn't plenty of others? And wasn't it perfectly possible that Max and these others were more concerned with the future success of Tony Lowder than Lee Lowder was? Even more unselfishly concerned? It was Max who had made Tony take the case of the communist professor which had got him such wide publicity and established his name in liberal circles. It was Max who had pushed his nomination for the State Senate. Max lived for Tony. And what about Joan Conway? Joan Conway was very ill, people said. She didn't look it, but there you were. People said she was, and rumors of serious illness, like rumors of marital discord, were usually true. Would she be glad if Joan died? No. On the whole, she thought she would be sorry. She liked Joan. She did not know that Joan was Tony's mistress. She only knew that Joan wanted to be. It was exceedingly curious that she did not care more about the exact nature of Joan's and Tony's relationship. She did not seem to be much bothered by so conventional a form of infidelity. Joan, after all, could not take from her, she was sure, that part of Tony that she held. No matter what things he did with Joan, he would make love just as often and just as well with his wife.

She saw Tony now crossing the room to her. It exasperated her that he was smiling, that he should assume so complacently that she would wait there patiently for him, that she would not rush out and take a cab home.

"Good news?" she asked coolly, knowing that his smile meant nothing in such matters.

"Well, we seem to need more money. We always seem to need more money."

"How will you get it?"

"I haven't a clue."

"Max, as your mother would put it, must have Daly blood."

"Why do you have it in so for Max tonight?"

"Because he's so . . . weak. Because he's not . . ." As she reached about for a word, she was surprised to find one that struck her as peculiarly apt. "Because he's not straight!"

Tony glanced up. "What makes you say that?"

"Well, didn't you tell me that when he represented Grace Nitter in her divorce from Joe he was really representing Joe? Who was afraid she'd go to some shyster who would fleece him?"

"Yes. But I was never sure to what extent it was a conscious misrepresentation on Max's part."

"I believe at the time you suggested that he had betrayed his client."

"Perhaps I did. But mightn't Grace have been

better off—from the point of view of her home and children—to have a little less in an amicable settlement than more in a filthy court battle?"

"That was her decision, not Max's."

"Well, I can't dispute that."

Lee saw her opportunity, as usual, washing off into the gutters of his eternal reasonableness. If she allowed herself to become cross, he would simply retreat into beneficent silence. Never had there been a man more impregnable to female attack.

"I don't know what your moral code is," she observed grumpily. "Or even if you really have one. You're always finding excuses for people like Max. Even when you know he's shifty and opportunistic."

"I try to understand him."

"Do you? Or do you try to think of him as something he's not? Something better? What do you really believe in, Tony?" It seemed to her that this was turning into a very odd conversation indeed, but she hurried on recklessly to plunge in deeper. "Do you believe in God?"

Tony folded his hands patiently on the table. "No."

She was surprised, even a bit disappointed. She considered herself an agnostic, but there always lurked in the back of her mind the possibility of some ultimate purpose, even of a final and rather funny joke of discovering, after all, an old-fashioned heaven with angels and harps. What a sell for the old clowns who were waiting for Godot. "Then, of course, you don't believe in an after-life."

"That's right. I believe this is all we have."

"And there's no point? To anything?"

"I don't see that follows. There's a point to being happy."

She felt unaccountably depressed and wondered if she should have a third drink. There seemed to be something sad in Tony's not having any faith. It was all right for *her* not to have any. That was different. God and his angels did not depend on the likes of her.

"What makes you happy?" she asked.

"I don't think I'd better tell you. It sounds so bloody fatuous."

Now her words came out with a sudden sob. "Oh, Tony, for God's sake, tell me. Can't you see I'm having a fit?" Strangest of all was his not finding her reaction undue. He even laughed at her.

"Oh, let's put it that I like to make you happy," he said. "There! Does that satisfy you?"

"No. You only married me because you felt sorry for me at that cocktail party. Because I was so blue about having a short story rejected by *The New Yorker.*"

"I married you because I fell in love with you. Because you were the most adorable and cutest creature in the world. And still are. You look just the same, you know. The same curly black hair. The same bright brown eyes."

"Oh, Tony, shut up!" She could not let him go on. She could not let him hypnotize her with clichés. She had not given up a literary career for *that.* But what literary career? She had had none, and she knew it. And he meant his clichés; he wasn't afraid of them. That was the terrible thing about him. "I think I will have a third drink, after all," she muttered.

3

Tony stood on the basketball court, twenty feet from the basket, holding the ball poised before him, studying the distance. A dozen boys of high-school age stood about, watching.

"Say, Tony, I've got a buck says you can't make two out of three."

"He did last week."

"Yeah? Some hot shot."

Tony threw the ball. It rose in a perfect arc and dropped through the basket without touching the ring.

"Jesus."

"How's that buck looking?"

"He can't do it again. Betcha."

One of them threw the ball back to Tony, and this time he tossed it without delay. A miss. He tried again. A miss. There was a pleased outburst of jeers.

"That's the Lowder style."

"A flash in the pan."

"Say, Tony, you lost that one like you lost the election."

"Say, Tony . . ."

"Say, Tony, do you know why you lost the election? My old man told me."

Tony had noted that since November they felt personally superior to him. An election was like a prize fight. The loser lost his balls. "What did your old man tell you, hot rock?" he demanded.

"He said you're always shooting your mouth off about blacks, but you send your kids to private school."

Tony shrugged. "Education's like anything else. The best costs the most. As long as I can pay, I'm buying the best."

"Jesus. How can you call yourself a liberal?"

"I can call myself anything I want, can't I?"

"My old man says you're a goddam wasp."

Tony flung up his hands in mock dismay. "My mother's Irish, and my father's part Jew. What are you trying to do? Kill me politically? I'm paying a genealogist to look for black blood."

There was a faint general snickering, and Tony's politics were dropped.

"Say, Tony. Is it true they're going to close down this goddam settlement house?"

"Say, Tony. Why don't you rich trustees fork over?"

"Rich?" Tony groaned. "I only come to committee meetings for the free lunch."

"Jesus. What a moocher."

"Say, Tony. Why don't you get the dough out of Mrs. Conway?"

"Yeah, Tony. They say that big broad's loaded."

"Say, Tony. Is it true you bang her?"

"Is she good, Tony?"

"Funny guys, funny guys," Tony muttered and hurried off the floor before Miss Hall, the director, who had appeared in the far doorway, should hear. Miss Hall had the handsome, sexless, marble looks of some professional old maids. Her extreme deference to trustees was never menial, simply formal.

"Oh, Mr. Lowder, I thought you'd gone. Mr. Leonard is in the board room. He was anxious to catch you."

"He always is."

"Tell me, do you think our treasurer was unduly gloomy?"

"I'm afraid not."

"Will we have to give up the summer camp?"

"Keep your fingers crossed."

"Oh, Mr. Lowder, if you could only talk Mrs. Conway into equaling her last year's gift."

"That was supposed to be a one shot deal. We can't expect her to support the house indefinitely."

"But you have such influence on her!"

Tony glanced back at the boys. Happily, they were playing ball again. "Besides, she's ill."

"Well, I suppose you know best." Miss Hall's true concern almost penetrated the brittle surface of her perfunctory affectations. "I wish all our trustees cared the way you do. It's wonderful the way you find the time to come here and play with the boys."

Tony turned from her brusquely. He could never abide compliments. "I'm a lousy trustee," he muttered. "A trustee should be able to give or get others to give."

"Oh, but you're a working trustee."

"There's nothing like money," Tony retorted.

As he mounted the long varnished stairway to the board room, he reflected how odd it still seemed to dread seeing Max. For years his life had been indissolubly bound up with that handsome baby face, those friendly sky-blue eyes, the shock of blond hair, the noisy ribald laugh. Max had been the spirit, the very soul of Lowder, Leonard, Bacon & Shea. And he had worked hard, too, for all his habit of reducing everything to jokes. That was what Lee could never see. Oh, perhaps it was true, as she never lost an opportunity of pointing out—women were relentless—that Max had used him and used his connection with the Conways, but had he not given it all back twice over? Who but Max had believed, from the beginning of their friendship as clerks in Hale & Cartwright, in what he had not scrupled to call Tony's "star"?

But now Max's show seemed over. The big, gay backdrop of his sybaritism had split down the middle, and all the gray frenzy of his industry was scattered over a darkened stage. Max had lost his head before he had even lost his money. He jumped up from the board table as Tony came in.

"This goddam recession!" he cried. "Nixon ought to be impeached. Herron's down another twenty points, and Everett wants his margin."

"How much?"

"Ten g's. From each of us."

"I haven't got it, Max. You know I haven't got it."

"And that's not all. We're going to need twenty more for Alrae before the end of the month. And there's the loan interest. Can't you get fifty from somebody? From Joan? From your family? It would get us through. It would even put us over.

Oh, Tony, don't look at me that way. Don't you see we could make it?"

Tony looked dispassionately at the pleading, oddly blank eyes that his friend thrust up at him, and at the tiny beads of sweat on the high, ivory forehead. Max was almost ugly when he was worried. Tony was surprised at his own coldness. This was the same Max, after all, to whom, a few weeks back, he had been so devoted.

"Max, is all this really worth it? Suppose we let it go?"

"Let it *go?*"

"Let the investment go. Take a bust. It doesn't have to be the end of the world, does it?"

"Doesn't it?" Max's voice was hoarse, and he looked about the room as if he suspected eavesdroppers. "We're up to the hilt, you and I. The firm's in it, too. We'd lose our office!"

"And what does that amount to?"

"The law library? The furniture? The lease?"

"Oh, to hell with them."

"To hell with them?" Max's eyes were brimmed now with actual tears of outrage. "To hell with bankruptcy? Do you think, Tony Lowder, for one solitary second, that you could be appointed to any government job if you and I went bust in a mess like this?"

Tony turned away impatiently. "You exaggerate. There's no disgrace in bankruptcy. Anybody can take a licking on this market."

"Dream on. When Governor Horton sees how much you've been gambling, he won't touch you with a ten-foot pole. You'll seem too giddy. At best."

"At *best?*"

"Well, there's something else."

"Come on, let's have it."

"I've borrowed from some pretty unsavory characters."

"Damn it all, Max!"

But Tony's sudden anger seemed only to excite Max to a final pitch of exasperation. "Damn it all yourself, Tony! Don't talk to me that way. Who the hell do you think you are? Who the hell do you think made the world aware that such a person as Tony Lowder even existed?"

"I guess I know what I owe you, Max."

Max's tone, at this small concession, slid at once from a screech to a whine. "Oh, I don't want your gratitude, Tony. I did it just as much for me as for you. The point is: we're a team. You're the star, sure, but the star still needs a manager. You're my big gamble, in politics, in law. Hell, in life. You're the only real, honest-to-goodness, in-it-to-the-finish friend I've ever had. We've got to stand together. And now . . . !" Max's whine suddenly subsided, and some of his old enthusiasm seemed to be rekindled in his eyes. "We're almost there, you know. We would have been, except for this filthy recession. Herron's basically sound; so are the restaurants. With anything like half a chance we could clear a million. We're so *close*, Tony. So close I can smell it. It's bust or glory. We could be all set, and you with a political career that could take you anywhere. Anywhere at all!"

Tony wondered why he did not care more. There was something eerie about the moments, like this one, when his ambition shut off, like the motor of an airplane, leaving him precariously to glide. One might have emotions; one might have sympathies; one might even have love, but without ambition it sometimes seemed that these other things simply jostled one aimlessly hither and yon, like eddying air currents, until the prevailing yank of gravity brought one to the inevitable smash.

"You talk as if I wanted to go broke," he said.

"Sometimes I think you do. You know Joan Conway would give it to you."

"Oh, lay off Joan Conway."

"Well, don't you!"

Max with this gave a howl of laughter and ran around the board table when Tony grabbed at him. Tony caught him and twisted his arm behind his back.

"Take it back."

"Oh, come on, Tony. Can't you even screw for money like that?"

Tony gave his arm an extra twist until Max squawked in pain and then let go in disgust. For Max actually liked it. His blue eyes had the fixed look of an ungulate overpowered by a carnivorous foe.

"You're a filthy-minded bastard," Tony said flatly. "However, I'll try to raise the money."

"That's talking."

"Mind you, Joan's only the last resort."

"I'm glad you can still talk of last resorts. Mine are all used."

"You should have stopped at the next-to-last."

"If I live, I'll learn. But do it for your kids, Tony. Do it for Lee."

"Why do you say that?"

"Because I haven't known you for fifteen years

without learning that the way to get something out of you is to appeal to your neurotic unselfishness."

"Get out of here."

••

Walking across the park to his parents' apartment house, Tony considered his "neurotic unselfishness." He had always been a bit embarrassed by this habit of preoccupation with the plights of others. It had seemed to turn the story of his life from the hard, clear lines of the kind of neoclassic drama that he had loved at college to a rosy Victorian tragicomedy, blurred by sentiment. It had kept him from establishing a proper distance between himself and his parents. And yet at the same time he knew that he judged them coolly enough. As a boy he had always been glad to get away from them, to school, to camp, to the houses of friends. Unlike most over-filial youths who turn their self-imposed duty into a pleasure or at least into an addiction, he obeyed its dictates only when they were clear. He seemed to have been at once strangely dominated and strangely free.

The ancient yellow-faced crone with stringy white hair who opened the door of the apartment, the combination cook and cleaning woman (Tony never knew why she worked for the wages Dorothy paid her) grumbled that his mother was out.

"I know, Nellie. I came early to have a word with Dad."

"Well, you'll find him where you always find him. Gawking into that goon-box."

Tony paused in the doorway. It was not a room that told one much about its occupants. His parents had added nothing to Dorothy's inherited furniture but certain latter-day necessities: the color TV set before which George Lowder passed his days, the gleaming nickel wheelchair which bore him to and from it, the encyclopedia and reference books that Dorothy had received as dividends from her book club. The rest was a faded reminder of the contractor ancestor's brief grandeur: two imitation Louis XV *bergères* with needlepoint seats and a worn Aubusson carpet. The room itself had too few windows and too many doorless doorways, like a stage set adapted to multitudinous exits and entrances.

George Lowder sat in his corner watching a baseball game. He was a poorly preserved seventy-eight. He had a bad heart, weak lungs and worse hearing, and he only rose from his wheelchair to take the few tottering turns about the room that his doctor required of him each morning and afternoon. Yet he managed to appear serene. His oblong face and near-bald scalp had acquired, in the torpid days of his terminal, interminable illness, a look of distinction quite inconsistent with the small facts of his biography. George appeared wise and benign, although in the days when he had still been able to get about he had struck people as possessing only the cheerfulness of the foolish and idle. If he had been painted fittingly in a conversation piece of the Lowder family, he would have been represented as a cipher. But by some miracle the cipher, at the end of its seventh decade, seemed to be filling out.

Filling with what? Tony wondered. Perhaps with a new independence of Dorothy. George had never apologized for earning no money, for producing nothing by way of substitute, for letting his wife bear the burden of bringing up the children and planning the household, but now he sometimes seemed on the verge of blaming her for reproaching him in these matters. He seemed to be implying, in the bland way in which he monopolized the television, or interrupted her talks with callers, or even contradicted her—oh, those high, gay, stubbornly repeated contradictions and that ineradicable smile—that if he was making a late stand, it was better late than never. Perhaps he believed that it would be a benefit to his children to glimpse the man he might have been had she not smashed him.

Tony shook his father's soft bony hand and leaned down to kiss his cheek. George's initial response, as always, was charming.

"Ah, Tony, my dear boy, how delightful to see you. But you're early. Your mother's not home yet."

"You must listen to me on Channel Thirteen tomorrow night," Tony told him. "I'm going to be on a panel discussing insiders and the stock market. What'll you give me not to stare right into the camera and say: 'Ladies and Gentlemen, I want you to know that my Dad, who's watching us right now, was one of the sharpest customers' men on Wall Street. Dad, this is the public. Public, this is Dad.' And then we could cut in your voice saying: 'The Public be damned.' "

"You wouldn't do that, Tony?" George asked in alarm. "That wouldn't be the thing at all, you know."

"Well, you'll never be sure I won't unless you watch. Tomorrow night at nine."

"Oh, that's bad luck. That's the time I watch the Ethna Pollock hour."

"Do you mean to tell me, Dad, that you wouldn't skip Ethna one night to hear *me?*"

"Well, the trouble is you don't get all the jokes in her program unless you keep up."

"I want you to hear me, Dad. I need your criticism."

"Very well, Tony, if you put it that way. Only you'll have to tell your mother to remind me. My memory's getting fearfully bad. I should forget my own head if it wasn't screwed on."

George's eyes kept reverting to the screen. It was not only that he didn't want to hear Tony in the future; he didn't want to hear him then.

"Look, Dad. I know it must be sad to grow old and feel that all your faculties aren't what they used to be. And I suppose you must have moments of feeling that you haven't accomplished all the things in life you wanted to. But the point is that all that any of us have, old or young, is *now.* It's just as important for you to be happy at seventy-eight as it is for Eric to be happy at twelve. I'd like to be closer to you. I'd like to understand you better." He paused. "I love you, Dad."

"Well, Tony, it's very nice of you to say that. You've always been a good boy. And a good son. Your mother's forever making a great point of that."

"You don't see it. I want to be a good son to *you.*"

"You are, Tony. You are. And now if you don't mind, I should like to go back to my baseball game. Can't watch and talk, you know."

Dorothy Lowder came hurrying into the living

room. "Tony, darling, if I'd known you were coming this early, I'd have been home. How much of you have I missed?"

She took him over to the sofa by the fireplace where they always talked, leaving George to his game. She never lowered her voice when she talked about her husband, depending on his deafness.

"Doctor Foster tells me he shouldn't be left alone even for a few minutes," she complained. "He says the next attack may come at any time. I'll have to get a day nurse or be chained to this apartment. Oh, Tony, how am I going to pay for it all?"

"Dip into capital."

"But I'm dipping."

"Dip more. Submerge yourself."

"But is it fair to you and Philip and Susan? After all, it was *my* father's money. He would never have wanted it all spent on George."

"Grandpa Daly didn't anticipate the high cost of medicine today. You have to be damn near a millionaire to afford a decently comfortable death."

"How can you make so light of these terrible things?"

"What should I do? Weep? Cheer up, Ma. You'll get through."

"No one cares the way you do, Tony. No one comes in so faithfully"

"I thought Susan came in regularly."

"Exactly! Regularly. I feel myself being checked off. And as for Philip, of course, he only comes when he wants money."

"Like me."

"Like you, darling? What on earth are you talking about? You never ask me for anything."

"I've been waiting." Tony watched her carefully, as suspicion began to creep into her eyes, suspicion rapidly followed by fear. "I have a proposition to put to you. Supposing you were to advance me a sum—a very large sum—against my ultimate share of your estate?"

"How large?"

"Well, say fifty thousand dollars."

"Tony Lowder! Tell me you're joking."

"Now, hold on, Ma. I would agree to pay you ten percent on that for your lifetime. That's twice what you're getting on it now."

"But where would *you* get that kind of return?"

"That's my affair."

"And what would my security be?"

"Me! Won't you gamble on me, Ma?"

"I'll do no such thing. I won't gamble on anything or anybody." Dorothy Lowder clutched her fists to her breast as if she anticipated his forcing them open to release hidden gold. "What have I had all my wasted life but the smitch of property my poor old father managed to put together for me? And you'd take that! You'd plunder your mother and reduce her to the state of one of those miserable hags you see rooting in garbage pails for old newspapers!"

Tony burst out laughing. "Don't worry, Ma! Of course, I couldn't take a penny after that. I was simply proposing the arrangement for your advantage. I can get my money in two or three other places."

Her half-open mouth and still pleading eyes suggested that she was torn between relief and the horrid suspicion that she might not have shown herself to best advantage. "I have to watch my money because of your father, of course," she hastened to explain. "Where would he be now, I'd like to know, if I hadn't kept together the little I have?"

"He'd be nowhere at all," Tony assured her. "You're absolutely right. And if ever again I come to you with a proposition about money I want you to promise me you'll kick my tail right out of here. Come on over to the desk, and I'll put it in writing."

"Oh, Tony dearest, you do see my point? You're not making fun of me?"

"Not a bit."

"Because I depend so on you. I couldn't bear it if you thought I'd denied you anything unreasonably."

"Forget it."

"Do you know what your brother Philip had the gall to tell me when I told him he should honor his father and mother? That there ought to be a statute of limitations for that commandment."

Tony laughed again. "That sounds like Phil."

"You make a joke of everything, Tony. Sometimes I wonder if you take anything seriously. What about this money you need? You're not in any real trouble, are you? I mean you haven't done anything . . . well, wrong, have you?"

"You mean do I need the money so I can put it back? Like my stealing those toys when I was twelve? No, Ma. Dad nipped my career in crime in the bud. I'm still pure as pure."

Dorothy got up now to put her arms around him, and he could feel her quickly beating heart. "Make us a drink, dearest," she said. "You've given me such a scare."

When Tony had gone, Dorothy felt again the full bleakness in the room and shivered. All her experiences in the past hour had been peculiarly physical. Tony had seemed to be sitting before her in a very corporeal sense, big, heavier than usual, very still. She had noticed the darkness of his chin and upper lip. Had he needed a shave? Something appeared to have gone out of him, or maybe it had gone out of him only for her. Had it, unbelievably, been a part of her love for him? Not her affection, of course, not her mother instinct, nor her preoccupation with him, nor even her nervous need to kiss him, to touch him, but some part instead of that wonderful, all-embracing, eye-closing, velvet-soft, heart-uplifting, soul-redeeming, life-giving adoration on which she had simply built her life. Had any of *that* gone out—even for a moment—with the sudden suspicion that he might have committed a crime? Oh, no, never, what did she care about what peccadillos in the crazy male world of silly stocks and boring bonds her darling boy might have committed? It was this new thing, this lunatic scheme to rob her that had shaken her to the roots. As the idea came back on her in all its horror, she even regretted that she had not taken him up on his offer to put his promise in writing.

"I think Tony looks tired," she said to George.

"Why shouldn't he? He must be in a peck of trouble to need all that money."

Dorothy looked up in surprise and saw that her husband's eyes had a malicious glint. "So you heard!"

"You don't treat your favorite son very well when he needs you, Dorothy."

"What do you think he's done?"

"Something crooked."

"George! The way you say that! You don't even seem shocked. Your own son, a crook!"

"My own son? What has that to do with it? Look whose grandson he is."

Dorothy stared, incredulous. "Are you referring to my father?"

"Who else? He had no moral backbone. Irishmen can withstand anything but temptation. Tony's the same way. I've always known it. Oh, I grant he's been a good boy, considerate and kind, the best thing your family ever produced, as a matter of fact. But he's still unable to stand up to any real temptation. I don't suppose he can help himself. It's in his blood."

What struck Dorothy most about this unprecedented harangue was that it seemed to be delivered quite without temper. George might have been discussing Tony's basal metabolism. He was emphatic—as if it were a point that he had made a thousand times over—but he was also bland. He sat there in his wheelchair, for all the world as if he were resting from a lifetime of successes, offering Olympian judgment on a son whom he seemed to regard so little his as to exempt him from all responsibility. Dorothy, searching frantically for a weapon to hurt him with, suddenly found it.

"You say that about Tony? Tony, who's the one child of yours who's ever cared for you?"

"I didn't say he wasn't a good son."

And he continued to blink at her. When he stopped at last and closed his eyes for a little nap he might have been the carcass of her family life.

4

Joan Conway's first reaction to the doctor's announcement that there was a recurrence of the cancer in her uterus only six months after the operation that was supposed to have cut it all out was one of passionate anger. It was too cheaply ironical, too vulgarly banal that at thirty-nine, with her beauty and her husband's fortune both still intact, she should face the prospect of imminent extinction. Oh, could she not see the complacent nodding, hear the complacent sighs. "Well, well, she thought she owned the world, didn't she? What good will her diamonds and her Louis XIII interiors do her now? Her sables and her cars? *Vanitas vanitatum!*"

He was young, Dr. Reid. Her old doctor had himself died of cancer. His successor was still embarrassed by death, though at least he knew enough to avoid the impertinence of sympathy. He spoke quietly as he seemed to study the card in his hand. Joan raged inwardly at the dimly lit room with its

Metropolitan Museum reproductions of Cézanne and Van Gogh, and its ghastly green furniture. Yet the wretched room would survive her.

"Will you operate again?"

"Probably. There'll have to be further tests."

"Is there any hope? No, skip that. I know the answer. There's always hope. I remember what Doctor Audreys said when I asked him if he told patients the truth. 'I don't have to. They don't want to know.' Well, neither do I."

"I never meant to imply there was no hope, Mrs. Conway."

"And I shan't ask you to. But promise me one thing, and I'll get my husband to endow a hospital for you. Promise me, if it's going to be long and painful—or even short and painful—that you'll give me something to finish it off."

"Mrs. Conway!" He stood up now, and his eyes, for all he could do to control them, *were* sympathetic, damn them! "You mustn't jump to such terrible conclusions. There are plenty of things we can still do. There's radium. We'll start treatments next week. I want you to come back to the hospital."

"When?"

"As soon as you can."

"I'll let you know."

"I have a room reserved for tomorrow."

"That's much too soon. I'll call you." She jumped up as she saw that he was about to protest. "I think I've had enough to today, Doctor, don't you? Forgive me."

She walked the ten blocks home up Park Avenue. Of course, it had to be a beautiful day, the sky a mocking blue. What else could she possibly expect from a world that, except for the old dead doting parents, had always viewed her with dislike and distrust? Oh hypocrite world that cared only for money and things and hated those who admitted to caring! Nature itself had been against her, for the womb that had denied her babies would now deny her life.

The apartment was empty except for Len, the perfect butler, who always knew when to be silent. Norry, thank God, was away on one of the constant business trips that nourished his illusion that his executive talents explained his vice-presidency on Conway & Son. The maids had the morning off because of the dinner party that night. She told Len that she would see no one, speak to no one, and then roamed the living room and library in consoling solitude. Did death exist if one were alone? She touched the bronze Italian figures on the tables; she fingered the Cellini cups; she placed the palms of her hands against the faces of marble statues. The way to leave such things? The way to leave the great Luke ruby glowing, warm, soul-warming, in the blue safe of her bedroom above?

People even criticized her taste. Imagine doing rooms in early seventeenth century! But Louis XIV, Louis XV were so trite. She loved the austerity of the linen fold paneling and of the tall, gaunt, straight-backed chairs which brought out the rich, exploding colors of the paintings: Vouet, Champaigne, Latour and the glorious Rubens. Some of the furniture would bring little enough at auction when Norry's next wife sold it, for Joan had pulled the divans apart to insert cushions and make them unexpectedly luxurious, but who cared? She had devised a home that would please at once the most confirmed aesthete and the most abandoned sybarite. It would never be appreciated, but what had been appreciated that *she* had ever touched?

She felt exhausted, but she knew it was only because of what Dr. Reid had told her. Lying down full length on a sofa she switched on her dictaphone and continued the memoirs that had been her only effective distraction since the advent of illness.

"Debutante year. 1949. The beginning and the end. The start of real life and the end of that life in reality. I was the last debutante of the western world. The last one, that is, to want to be a debutante, to believe in being a debutante. To believe that it was a great and thrilling and wonderful thing to be a debutante. Not that I ever admitted it, oh, no! I was not such a fool. I knew the fashion. I knew one had to play down the debut, question its worth, voice a preference for travel or work among the lowly. I knew one had to swear one went through it only to please one's family. Yet the fiendish thing about philistines is that for all their crudeness and for all their insensitivity, they somehow manage to smell one out. They *knew* I wanted to be a debutante. That I believed in being a debutante. And they feared and hated me for it."

Joan's eyes were wet at the picture of the lonely, angry girl that she had been. She wondered if there were anything in her life she would have done differently, given the chance. Would they have hated her less?

"Except Mummie and Daddy. Poor darling dowdy old Mummie and Daddy. How ashamed I was of them and how much I miss them! If I have deserved this cancer, it was for treating them as I did. Oh, I was good enough to them after I married Norry, but everything was easy then. Before, in that long before, I suffered tortures over Mummie's dumpy figure, her fussy clothes, her misplaced kindliness, her big lugubrious features, her fatiguing loquacity, her habit of inadvertently sitting with her knees apart so everyone could see her old white flabby thighs—and more. And Daddy's horrible fatness, his silly laughter, his watery eyes, his bad breath. I saw how they bored the world. I even saw that they saw it themselves. They hung on to their poor little peg of social position and accumulated the income of Daddy's scrap of a trust, all for the glory of their phoenix of a debutante daughter. They toddled about the fashionable watering places; they plucked elbows and murmured in ears; they suffered the crudest rebuffs, just to make themselves soft ashes from which *I* could rise. Ah, poor darlings, it is almost worth believing in extinction just to know that you can't see me now."

She wondered if she cared if anyone should ever play the tape. Norry? Why should she care? Why should he? What was left but truth?

"Why did everyone see through me? Did I allow mockery to slip into the service that my lips rendered? Was it that the pale, pasty beauty that I affected, set in a frame of long raven hair, was too reminiscent of the era of real debutantes? Why did even poor Norry, that last fruit of the Pittsburgh tree so long plucked by New Youk virgins, suspect me of mercenary motives? Why did I so nearly lose him to that little brown bundle of spite, Mamie Rivers, who was somehow able to veil her own passion for gold behind her own bright eyes? Oh, but they couldn't resist me; Norry couldn't resist me. Even knowing me they couldn't resist me, and, damn them all, whatever happens, I've had the world—I've had the whole goddam glittering world. It's not much, God knows, but it's better to have had it than to have had nothing! Nothing, anyway, but cant and hypocrisy and the pretense of living for anyone but your own sole, solitary, bitchy, selfish self."

She switched off the machine as she saw Len in the doorway. "Blast you, Len, what do you want?"

"Sorry, Ma'am. Will you speak to Mr. Lowder?"

"Of course, I'll speak to Mr. Lowder." She sat up and picked the gray telephone out of the linen-fold box. "If you're telling me you're not coming for dinner, Tony, I'll never forgive you."

"It's not that," his voice replied. "Lee just phoned to say she has flu."

"But you're coming?"

"Unless that puts your table out."

"Kid on. Look, Tony, come early, will you? Tell Lee I've changed the hour to seven."

"She'll never believe that."

"Well, then tell her it's business. God damn it, I'm a client, aren't I? Just because you've gone into government doesn't mean you can throw me over. I'll see you at seven. Not a minute later."

Tony's voice became stubborn. "You think just because you helped finance my campaign, you can order me around."

"Damn right I do."

"Well, think again."

She changed her tone to a mocking whine. "All

right, Albert, it's not the Queen. It's Vicky, your loving wife. Now will you come? Please?"

When he had rung off, Joan felt better. If there had been no afternoon to fill until dinner time she might have been almost content. There was something about Tony that always dispelled fear—probably the simple fact that he was immune to it. While she was with him, she shared some of his immunity. And she could sleep until six. She had a pill for that.

••

At eight o'clock the big room, brightly lit, smelled agreeable of incense. Joan, in white, wearing her rubies, drinking a glass of undiluted gin, pretended for a while to listen to Tony's political chatter.

"I feel so content and secure," she interrupted. "Do you ever feel content and secure? All of a sudden? As if you and I existed all alone and nobody else was really real?"

"I feel that way sometimes after I've drunk as much as you have. What's got into you tonight, Joan? Your guests will be here in a minute."

"I don't care. I don't worry. Do you ever worry?"

"Oh, yes."

"Over what?"

"Oh, over something that you haven't had to worry about for many a year."

"Money, I suppose."

"How you say that! As if it were something trivial, faintly absurd. Even contemptible."

"It is. Believe me, Tony. It is. It's worse. It's a bore."

"Then why not get rid of it?"

"It's not mine. It's Norry's. Oh, I have a little, of

course. Would you like it? Shall I give it to you?" Tony was pushing the crystal ashtray on the table back and forth in a gesture of impatience. "But I mean it," she protested. "It's not just the gin. You're my only real friend, and I love you. Why should you be worried when I have money? Why should I not share it with such a friend? How much do you need?" Tony, however, continued to brood. "Seriously, lover, how much?"

"Perhaps I could accept a loan," he muttered.

"Certainly. Speak to Mr. Nash at the bank. I'll tell him to do anything you say."

"I don't want you to think I'm going to grab the moon. Forty thousand would be a Godsend. Forty thousand for three months."

The specificity of his need was like a cold rag rubbed suddenly into her face, and she was back in Dr. Reid's office with the cheap reproductions of Van Gogh. She trembled all over. Tony watched her change of expression with surprise. Then he shrugged.

"I see how it is," he said, now sullen. "You want to help, but you hate me for needing it. You rich all belong to the same club. You're better off sticking with each other."

"Do you know that I may be dying?"

"Jesus, Joan!"

"It's come back."

"Joan!" He did not move or even take her hand, but she felt the shock of his sympathy and was instantly better. "How bad?"

"That bad. I don't know. I don't want to talk about it. I'll be going back to the hospital for treatment. Maybe I'll be all right. Maybe not. Oh, who *cares*? Just don't talk about it."

"Look, Joan. I wasn't serious about that loan. Lee and I made a bet last night. She said you were like all rich people. That you gave oodles of money to charity but hated giving it to friends. She said you were actually afraid of giving it to friends. As if their poverty might be catching."

"Lee said that?"

"Yes, but she was wrong, and I win the bet. I tested you, and you immediately offered me the money. I was simply picking a quarrel to get out of it when you broke up my little game with this hideous news."

Len appeared in the doorway and nodded to Joan.

"Oh, damn it, Tony. The first guest. I don't know if I should believe you, but I'm going to. I've got to." And suddenly, as she rose, she knew that she did believe him. "Oh, Tony," she murmured as she saw two figures behind Len, "don't leave tonight until they've all gone. Don't leave me."

Now he did take her hand, publicly, gravely, in front of the approaching couple.

"I promise."

Tony outstayed all the guests and went to Joan's bedroom after the household had left and Len had turned out the hall lights. It was not very satisfactory, for Joan was fuzzy with drink, but it was wonderful that he spent the whole night with her, holding her in his arms. In the morning she did not even ask him how he would explain his absence to Lee. She felt sure now that he could explain anything. Or that he did not have to. She telephoned Dr. Reid to say that she was ready to go to the hospital.

5

Nothing that Max Leonard was hearing on the telephone matched the bright yellow cheerfulness of his Madison Avenue office in Lowder, Leonard, Bacon & Shea (or Leonard, Bacon & Shea, as they would have to call it now that Tony had gone into government). Nor did the news that his broker offered fit with the colorful marine prints on his walls: the *Monitor* firing away at a hulky *Merrimac* and the *Constitution* in full sail on a blue, blue sea. Or with the silver-framed photographs of Max and the great, sometimes in color, of Max, young, blond and smiling, always the boy, seen behind Mayor Lindsay on a platform, or by Tony at Madison Square Garden, or dancing at a fund-raising dinner with Sophia Loren. Or with the certificates of all the courts to which Max had been admitted or with the page, extracted and framed, from the Williams College yearbook of eighteen years back showing Max, looking only slightly younger, over a legend that represented the verdict of his peers:

"If Max strikes you as only a good time Johnnie, watch out! The guy's a dynamo disguised as sugar candy!"

"I'm sorry, Max," Bob Everett went on, "Things are tough all over. Do you think you're the only margin buyer who's been caught in this recession? Herron Products is still down, and I still need twenty g's to cover you and Tony."

"Where am I supposed to get it?"

"What about that limited partnership you went into? The Jersey restaurant deal?"

"Alrae? If we don't get a bank loan before the end of the month, that's down the drain, too."

"What about your law firm?"

"Joke? When did small law firms have that kind of cash?"

"Can't Tony go to the Conways?"

"Tony *won't* go to the Conways. She's sick. He says he's been to everybody he can go to."

"Then he can go broke."

"Jesus, Bob! You know how close we are to a breakthrough. Why can't you see us through yourself?"

"Myself! Hell, man, I'm in the same boat!"

"Sometimes I wonder if we couldn't get an injunction to make Nixon stop this crazy war that's scaring the market."

"You do that. You do just that. In the meantime I'll be selling you out."

"Give me at least till Monday, for God's sake."

"Why? Will you have it Monday?"

"I've always had it before, haven't I?"

There was a long pause, followed by Everett's sigh of exasperation.

"Okay. Till Monday. But you know I shouldn't."

Max folded his hands in quiet misery as he stared into the big empty crystal inkwell above his blotter and cursed the war, the government and the bad luck of Max Leonard. He felt suddenly depleted, as if a lifetime of running just ahead of due dates had at last presented him with the bill. But hadn't he always known it would? That his luck couldn't hold forever? That the whole hysterical forty-year cycle of being something one was not—or at least never quite—the brightest and most popular boy in his class, the proud young husband of the prettiest girl in hers, the brilliant lawyer, and fixer, the handler of situations, the manager of the rising spokesman of liberals—had to end when the energy, or daring, or capacity of self-delusion, or, again, the possible just plain luck, ran out? He had been able to pay off the creditors of youth who had backed him through law school and marriage to Elaine by the unanticipated early death of his mother, who had left him *just* enough. He had been able to pay off the second group, those who had staked him to the handsome law office that had enabled him to lure Tony Lowder from Hale & Cartwright by going behind Tony's back to Tony's client, Joan Conway. But there was such a thing, obviously, as the end of the road. And yet. It was like a dream where you run and run and run, and there it is, the goal, the rostrum, the prizes, the hum already of the applause, but you can't *quite* reach it, you can't ever reach it. Tony in politics at last, and just as Max had seen and planned, a hit, and the money almost theirs—the very brink of glory—and now this. Max would have to look for a job as a wretched law clerk. At best.

He looked resentfully at Elaine's heart-shaped

face and lustrous hairdo on the other side of the empty inkwell. Elaine's marriage vows had been strictly for richer or richer. She would not even try to understand failure. Well, let her go. Let her take the children and go back to her snippy old mother. That was the least of his worries. The one insane error of his whole career had been to marry a poor girl, and yet it had seemed logical at the time, indeed imperative. For Elaine had been herself just as much the symbol of success as the money that he had wanted. What was the good of one without the other?

But what was the good of either? Might there not be an actual relief in failure? That was the way Tony sometimes talked. Tony talked to him about Max Leonard as if Max Leonard did not understand the contradictions of his own nature. This was absurd because crazy people usually know they're crazy. Max was utterly aware of his own craziness, aware of it from minute to minute, aware of all his drives and compulsions, aware of the hopelessness of it all. He knew that the brief dizzy moments of joy when one of his plans worked out were hardly worth the fuss. But what else could a man do? He picked up the ringing telephone.

"What is it, Miss Jordan?"

"It's that man again, sir. The one you spoke to yesterday who wouldn't give his name."

"I'll take him." He quickly pressed the white button. "Good morning, Jerry."

"Okay, fella, where is it?"

"I haven't got it."

"I didn't ask you that. I asked, where is it?"

"I need time, Jerry."

"I don't give time. You know that."

"What can I do then?"

"You guess what *I* can do, fella. You guess."

"I'm sure I don't know."

After a pause, Jerry Lassatta's voice was the least bit flatter. "Guess."

"Jerry, I've got a client waiting. Can I call you back?"

"Are you kidding?"

"No, seriously. It's a client I might get some money out of."

"See that you do. I'll call back in an hour."

When he hung up, Max was so frightened that he thought that he was going to vomit. Then he struck out wildly with his fists as if his fear were an antagonist that could be pushed away. He had to jump up when Miss Jordan came suddenly into the room with the mid-morning mail.

"Get out!" he shouted.

"Well! I certainly will!" she retorted. She would probably leave now. He didn't care. He didn't even mind alienating and losing a perfect secretary. He slammed his door after her and locked it.

Fear nullified life, stripped out the lining and the color, made love and laughter mockeries. He remembered reading of a crewman in a bomber who had tried to jump from the plane under anti-aircraft fire because he preferred death to the fear of death. How he understood that now. It had never occurred to him, when he had started borrowing from Jerry Lassatta, that he would ever be treated as the debtors of loan sharks are treated. He was too grand. Lassatta was too grand. For Lassatta, he had known from the start, was far more than the president of a truckers' local. That was only a front. Lassatta, whom he had met while canvassing labor leaders for Tony, was a power in the underworld, in the Mafia . . .

"Guess," Lassatta had said.

Would ugly, bullet-headed men be seen lurking about the house in Vernon Manor? Would Elaine be troubled with odd telephone calls, with strangers in the street who addressed her with unbecoming familiarity and asked her how "Maxy" was? Would he be tripped up at night and beaten to pulp? Would he be flung in the East River, his feet in a cement box? No, no, probably not—it was all too ridiculous—but how would he ever feel safe again, and what was life worth under the hair shirt of this hideous fear? Maybe he would be safe in Tony's apartment, with Tony. In Tony's arms. What an image! But now he was crazy, crazy with fear! Tony, of course, did not know what fear was. Fear might not exist in the presence of the fearless. Oh, why had Max been born such a miserable thing as a man, a man whom a boy had to grow into or die, a man who had to be always doing something or feeling something—or not feeling something, not feeling fear? Why could he not have been a girl, a pretty girl like Elaine, or like Lee, and turn from a terrible world into the wide, dark, enfolding embrace of Tony Lowder?

Tony, Tony, save me!

Miss Jordan's pouting voice sounded on the telephone. "That man's on the wire again."

"Yes, Jerry?" he said into the instrument. "Can't you even give me an hour?"

"I'm at Canal Street. Meet me at Gridley's Bar. Don't sweat. I've got a proposition."

Half an hour later, from the doorway of the dark bar and grill, Max spotted Lassatta across the room. The latter did not seem to be watching for anyone. Indifferent, impassive, oddly gentle looking, he smoked a cigarette and stared straight ahead. He still looked the friendly soul he had once seemed, short and stout with round, bland face, stubby, curly black hair and eyes that were humorous when they were not suddenly opaque, remote. Jerry could talk on any topic in the world, but he talked like a man from Mars, not really concerned. He could be amused, cynical; he could be occasionally funny, but he never seemed to regard the subject—be it war, peace, prosperity, depression—as having anything essential to do with him, Jerry Lassatta, or with reality. Max closed his eyes and prayed for the Jerry he had first known.

Then he walked across the room and sat down at the table. Jerry smiled.

"Hi, pal," he said. "What'll you drink?"

6

Tony had been silent for ten minutes, standing by the window in Max's office, looking down at the long, gray, slug-like bus tops that nudged their way to the curb. When he spoke, his tone was the least bit mocking.

"So here we are already. On the threshold of crime."

Max glanced toward the closed door. "You mustn't shout about it. I'm not even sure it's a crime. It's quite unprovable, anyway—a nonfeasancy kind of thing."

"I won't insult your legal intelligence by bothering to repudiate that. I'll simply attribute it to the pressure you've been under." Tony strolled over to Max's desk and looked down at him. He felt the same detachment that he had felt in the Settlement House, the same mild contempt. "Gosh, man, you do look done in. It's the first time I've ever seen circles under those famous boyish blue eyes.

You should be more careful. Your juvenile charm is one of our trademarks."

"Can it, Tony. This is serious."

"What's so serious about it? Why, your hands are actually trembling! What are you afraid of, pal? You don't think these thugs will actually do something to you?"

"Well, they're not renowned for their gentleness."

"You're afraid they might rough you up? Forget it. That's the kind of treatment they reserve for the two-bit storekeeper who's lost his interest money playing the horses. Lassatta didn't lend you money because he wanted your thirty percent. That was just an incidental benefit. He lent you money to get you in a hole so he could get at *me*."

"But I'm still in the hole, aren't I?" Max looked down at his shaking hands. "Tony, please let's do it and get out of this mess. Please, Tony!"

"Take it easy."

"You don't know these guys. They're not afraid of anyone or anything. They'd bump off John Lindsay himself if he was in their way."

"Oh, Max!"

"They would! But, all right, don't think of the negative aspect. Think of the positive. Look at it this way. We get the time we need. We get the money. With any luck at all, we'll break through into some kind of real dough. And you don't have to do anything. That's the beauty of it. You don't have to take any risk or commit any crime. You leave everything to me. Isn't that simple enough? And in six months' time you're on your way to becoming .. well, you name it, Mr. Commissioner."

Tony walked slowly back to the window where he stood looking out again, stroking his chin. He had a funny feeling of being excited all around his heart—so that the muscles in that area seemed painfully tightened—and at the same time of being calm, even numb, in all other parts of his body. The great thing had to be not the money, but the experience. Yet what value could there be in any experience that had to be shared with anyone as spiritually degraded as Max now seemed? "I concede the beauty of the plan," he said at last. "It's quite admirable, really. Let me go over it again, step by step, to be sure I have it all straight."

"Go ahead."

"Menzies, Lippard and Company are in trouble. They're undercapitalized by a million and a half. If they don't meet the SEC requirements by a week from Friday, they're suspended from trading on the stock exchange. That means they're shut down. Finished."

"And the *Menzies* case is on your desk."

"Obviously, it has to be. Now let me go on. Lassatta owns or represents a good piece of Menzies, Lippard. We're not sure which. Perhaps he's a limited partner through a front name. Perhaps the chief of his Mafiosan family is. It doesn't matter. The point is that Lassatta stands to lose heavily, personally or as a representative, if Menzies shuts up shop next week. But if I manage to sit on the case so as to give them more time—for two more weeks to be exact—which is all Menzies thinks he needs to raise his money—then forty g's of crisp new bills will be slipped to Max Leonard in an envelope while he is urinating in some washroom."

"The graphic details are yours."

"Ah, yes, something must be, I suppose. As you say, I am to take no risk. I don't even have to arrange the delay. All I have to do is *not* do anything about the Menzies matter for two weeks. It would look, at worst, like simple laziness. Or, at best, like the exercise of enlightened judgment. I shall have used my discretion to avoid the disastrous failure of a distinguished brokerage house. I might even be a hero."

"You're very funny."

"I'm very grave."

Max leaned forward and covered his face. "Can't you ever be serious?"

"Don't despair, my friend. I haven't turned you down yet. But in a matter like this I insist on dotting every 'i' and crossing every 't'. What kind of a devil are you if you won't let a man discuss the soul you're trying to buy? If I am to become a bribed civil servant, Max Satanicus, I am going to become it with my eyes very wide open."

"But I know you when you take that tone," Max retorted wearily. "It always means you've decided against something."

"Do you know me? If you did, you'd know that your proposition intrigues me. It intrigues me immensely. If I'm ever to commit a crime, it strikes me that this might be the right one." Tony paced up and down the rug as he worked it out. "Look at each aspect of it. Where is the wrong? Where is the hurt? Start with the bribe money. Where does it come from? The public? No. The government? No. It comes from the Mafia. Whatever you and I did with it would be at least as socially valuable as what they would. So no loss there. And if Menzies, Lippard is saved from closing, is that not for the public benefit? Are not hundreds of innocent investors saved from possible insolvency? So far so good. But what about Lassatta, or whoever he represents? Wouldn't it be better if they lost their investment in Menzies? Not necessarily. Because this is probably a retirement account. The Mafiosi, like other prudent persons, save for rainy days and senility and terminal ailments. And if they lose their savings, don't they have to go back to robbing and killing for more?"

For the first time in their session Max seemed to be thinking of something besides his own panic. "You don't have to go so far as to make out that we're public benefactors!"

"Why not?" Tony exclaimed. "If everything comes out for the better? Now, let us consider the intangibles. Do we, by taking this bribe . . ."

"*I* take the bribe."

"Nonsense, Max. I'm the public officer. Do we, by taking this bribe, decrease respect for the United States Government? No, because nobody will know of it but a couple of crooks who have no respect for government anyway. And, as far as you and I are concerned, you will have been relieved of a cruel anxiety, and the temptation to do further wrong, while I shall have been placed in possession of means through which to become a better public servant."

"So what is lost?" If Tony had to be humored, Max's expression seemed to say, well let him be humored.

" 'Nothing but honor,' as Jim Fisk put it. That, of course, is lost forever. And I won't try to delude you by quoting Falstaff. We should have indeed lost something when we have lost honor. But precisely what that amounts to is for *us* to decide. We should have made a choice, of our own free will, and for motives that we have thoroughly explored, to commit a criminal act. We should be in charge of our destiny."

"You mean you'd do this thing as some kind of an intellectual game?"

"If you want to put it that way."

Max shook his head and sighed. "You're only playing with me. You'll never go through with it."

"I haven't decided."

"Oh, but you have."

"I haven't. I'll go for a walk. I'll go to the zoo. And tomorrow, I'll let you know. Will that be time enough?"

Max showed at least that he could still laugh. "Don't be eaten by the lions," he cried. "Don't be a martyr to your own non-God."

7

Tony walked in Central Park for an hour, but he found it unexpectedly difficult to bring his mind to any considered appraisal of Max's proposition. It was like walking resolutely down a long corridor to a particular door and placing one's hand firmly on the knob only to be distracted, before turning it, by some fool at the end of the corridor shouting one's name or perhaps by some fool just shouting. At one point, by the boat pond, watching the elaborate model of a schooner making its precarious way across the water, he wondered in despair if it would be possible for him to do any thinking about Max's plan at all. And it was sufficiently extraordinary that he could not even make out whether the procrastination of his mental processes was operating for or against the plan.

Sitting on an empty bench, he tried putting the question to himself aloud: "Are you going to do what Max proposes?" Then he opened his lips to let the answer emerge, as if by some process of free association. None came. Was there no idea, no image in his mind? None but the banality that one crime must lead to another? "What rot," he exclaimed aloud. Why should he have to assume the very proposition that he sought to rebut: that man was not free? Man was free. Free to commit one crime, or two, or three—or none.

He decided that he might think better in company and went home. It was six o'clock, and Lee and both children were having their daily argument in the living room. Isabel greeted him with her usual passionate appeal.

"Mummie's been criticizing the young. She says we don't get any joy out of life. That we're discouraged before we're even started. But she won't see that's only one side of the picture. We're discouraged because we *care*. We care about people being shot and tortured and starved all over the world. I think we're going to be known as the 'moral generation.'"

Tony stared at the girl as though she had just penetrated his secret. Then he laughed. "Why moral? It's just a fashion, isn't it?"

"Oh, Daddy! A fashion?"

"Sure. Don't you think our descendants may look back on our worrying about ghettos and racial prejudice the way we look back at Catholics worrying about Luther?"

"No! Worrying about people's religion was silly."

"You say that because you've never had any religion," Eric put in.

"Well, have *you*, Eric?" his father asked.

"Perhaps not. But I see that churches may have the right idea. They go in for absolutes. Isabel's full of sentimental goo."

"Oh, Eric, you and your absolutes. You're nothing but a Nazi."

"Children!" Lee protested. "Your father hasn't put in a long day at the office to come home to this."

Tony looked at her as he had just looked at Isabel. Did she see it too? But he was much too touchy. "No, it's all right, I like it," he said easily. "It's funny to consider all the things we do perfectly freely, even thoughtlessly, that we could have been burned alive for a few hundred years ago. Think of all the peccadillos the Holy Office used to punish so hideously. Think of the tongues that were cut out for slandering public officials and the men who were jailed for unionizing. And when we come to sex . . ."

"I believe," Lee interrupted drily, "that in some benighted eras a man could even be put to death for making love to another man's wife."

Tony turned to her, straight-faced. "Surely there couldn't have been many who did anything as wicked as that."

"Oh, Daddy!" Isabel exclaimed scornfully. "You're not with it at all. That happens all the time. Now we heard at school that Mary Burton's father . . ."

"Isabel!" Lee protested. "That's enough. Now will you both please go to your rooms and finish your homework. You can come back and sit with Daddy while we've having supper."

Tony went to the bar table to mix the cocktails. He was suddenly elated by the discovery that he could be two persons at once—two happy persons. All his life, it seemed, he had been afraid of not being the person whom his loved ones loved. He had shared the common human suspicion that if his mother, his wife, his friends could once peek behind the mask that he (and perhaps everyone else) wore, they would no longer love the person so revealed to them. And so, with total revelation, human love would disappear from the globe, except perhaps Tony Lowder's, for it was his peculiarity to like people's faults. But now it struck him that even if Lee would not have loved the Tony behind the mask, it did not have to matter so long as the mask remained. Two Tony Lowders could exist simultaneously and with equal reality: the Tony Lowder who was conventionally honest and whom Lee Lowder loved, and the Tony Lowder who was a crook and whom Lee Lowder might not have loved. He even began to feel the possibilities of continued exhilaration in the manipulation of these two Tonys.

When he brought Lee her drink, she told him the big news of the day. "Governor Horton called. He said he'd tried your office, but you were out. He wanted you to know that he hadn't forgotten you. He said if he couldn't wangle the SEC, he might be able to get you an assistant secretaryship at the Treasury. Oh, Tony, would we move to Washington?"

He felt a throb of pity as he made out the urgency in her eyes. Lee had filled out a bit with the years, and there was a hint, just a hint, of middle-aged dumpiness in her hips and shoulders, but her snubby, turned-up nose, her large brown watery eyes, her curly black hair, her desperate intensity, all contributed to preserve the sentimental image of the little girl that held his imagination in so tight a vise.

"I didn't know you loved Washington."

"Oh, darling, we need a change. We've been marking time ever since the election. We haven't gone back to the old life, and we haven't really started a new one. I want you to get on with your political career. I want you to get on with the job of becoming a great man."

"Since when did you become so ambitious?"

"I'm not in the least ambitious—you know that. It's just that I've finally seen what you must become. And that we've all got to help you become it."

"Or else?"

"Or else?" She shrugged as if this were a matter of no conceivable importance. "Or else we miss the boat. I don't know how much that matters, but, generally speaking, boats should not be missed."

"And when did you decide all this?"

She looked at him keenly for a moment, as if she were about to say something for which she might be punished. "That night you went to Joan's for dinner and didn't come home."

"You never mentioned that."

"No, but I imagine my silence was thunderous."

"Would you like to hear what happened? Joan's desperately ill, you know."

"I *do* know. And I don't in the least want to hear what happened. If you tell me you only sat and held her hand all night, I'll be disgusted. And if you tell me something else, I'll be equally disgusted. Let us leave it that a gentleman has to do what a dying lady asks."

He tried to make out what she was feeling from the fixed half-smile in her eyes. He knew that smile, and he knew that it could mean different things.

"Very well," he agreed. "But what does that have to do with me and politics?"

"I did a great deal of thinking that night. I began to see that I had made a mistake—the commonest mistake that women make—in trying to get hold of you. In trying to be part of you or own part of you. It's so banal, so vulgar, that eternal clutching after a man, to avoid the bathos of loneliness. To avoid the basic human job of learning to live with oneself. Soul fleeing—that's what we're always doing. Running away from our own souls." She seemed to be working herself up to an actual fit of temper with herself. "I realized at last that being jealous of Joan was batting my head against a wall. That if it wasn't Joan, it would be somebody else. Or something else. For what I began to see was that Joan wasn't all sex. That she's not unlike politics to you."

"Well, of course, she's been a great contributor."

"Oh, I don't mean that. I mean that she's part of a crowd. The crowd that plays such a large role in your consciousness. The crowd that logically, sensibly, may one day become your constituents. The crowd of which I, like Joan, can be a part. The only way one can become a part of somebody else is by becoming a part of the thing they're part of."

Tony shook his head. "You're angry with me."

She stepped up and threw her arms about him. "Darling, I'm not. Believe me, I'm not. I'm trying so hard to be good and sensible. And to be happy. That's the point."

"You're right. That *is* the point."

"And I've been thinking. I don't want you to give that extra time to me and the children I used to ask for. That was being as bad as your mother. I was only thinking of myself. I want you to get on with your career. Full time. And I want to help you. All the way."

Her eyes were pleading, sincerely pleading. Whatever her motive, she had certainly convinced herself. Had he reached the point where he expected her to convince *him?*

"I will, Lee."

Later that night, after she had gone to sleep, he lay awake, trying to take in the fact of what he had decided to do. For how could he now tell that trusting girl that her new hopes for him, on which she was building a new life for her loving heart, were to end in his political failure and bankruptcy? As the hours went by and he lay stiller than he could ever remember lying on a sleepless night, he tried to fight the persistently encroaching idea that what was going to happen on the morrow was a birth, the birth, forty-three years delayed, of Anthony Lowder. For up until now, it more and more struck him, he had existed like something floating in space, subject entirely to the attraction or repulsion of other objects that happened to come within his sphere. Now something was happening within himself. A little muffled motor, deep in the recesses of his psyche, had started to revolve, to throb, to whir. Anthony Lowder was going to start his own motion in a black void, and it could hardly matter where that motion took him. Success or failure were less important than the fact that he was making his own decision—independently and unsentimentally. The only thing that created a small doubt was the idea, implanted by Max, that he might be going to commit the crime for the sake of committing it—to round out and perfect his own little squalid existentialist story.

After three in the morning he fell asleep and dreamed that he had done what Max had proposed. It was a curious dream in that what he had done varied in no particular way from what he and Max had discussed that afternoon. It seemed not so much a dream as a rehearsal. When he awoke, he was drenched in the sweat of relief that it was only a dream.

"Perhaps it's a warning," he told his haggard reflection as he shaved. "Perhaps I had better give up the whole thing."

And then he smiled because it occurred to him that he was afraid. Would there never be an end to sentimentality? When would he learn it was not a question of courage or manliness or morality but simply of choice?

Before Lee or either of the children was awake he went into the living room and dialed Max's number.

8

Tony at fourteen had had a religious experience. At least for almost four years he believed it to have been one. It was never repeated, but its effect on him was nonetheless powerful. It followed what he always afterward considered his initiation in crime.

His younger brother's passion in life was a dolls' house. Philip at twelve was a large fat boy with black greasy hair and a shrill, aggressive disposition. He refused to make the smallest compromise with a world that largely bored him. He liked the movies; he liked to exchange dirty stories with a small number of unattractive friends; he liked to play with and embellish the elaborate dolls' house that he maintained in his bedroom in the Riverside Drive apartment.

This dolls' house was a cause of constant mortification to his parents, particularly to his mother who knew too well with what glee the Dalys must have discussed the masculine deficiency which it represented. She banished it to Philip's room and refused to buy him dolls or furniture for it. But Philip, who derived a dusky delight in flinging in hostile faces the unorthodoxy of his pleasures, dragged visitors in to see his treasure and caused a mocking hilarity at family gatherings by loudly specifying the miniature ornaments that he needed as his Christmas or birthday due. Dorothy Lowder found, like many censors before her, that she had only exposed her shame to the spotlight. Tony decided that Philip should have one ally in the family.

He had to break down the natural distrust of the maverick for the regular fellow, of Mummie's cross for Mummie's darling. An older brother, unlatching the side of the dolls' house for a peek, must have seemed the most Trojan of horses. But Tony was persistent, and Philip, for all his snarling independence, needed a friend. When Tony promised to get him a French divan for the dolls' house parlor, Philip was interested.

"But how will you get it? They're very expensive."

"I might ask Grandpa Daly. He promised me five dollars for swimming that mile last summer. He never paid up."

"He never will!" Philip snorted in derision. Grandpa Daly, the family god, had clay feet to the younger generation. "Besides, he hates my dolls' house."

"Well, what he doesn't know won't hurt him."

But Tony got nowhere with Grandpa Daly, who gave him a lecture on the poverty of his own childhood in County Cork, and anyway he had discovered just the divan that he wanted for Philip, which was not to be had for money. It was a beautiful little green French sofa in the splendid dolls' house of Inez Feldman, only daughter of a rich Jewish banker who occupied a baroque mansion just north of the Lowders' apartment house. Inez was a fat, spoiled, opinionated brat with a snooty smile and pigtails, and she didn't give a hoot about any of her many things, but that didn't mean she would give them away. She liked Tony, but when he had asked her to make him a present of an old Howard Pyle book that she never looked at, she had turned him down flat, saying it had been a present from a favorite uncle. He knew her type. Things acquired a value in Inez's eyes simply by being coveted by others.

Tony was certain, however, that she would never miss the sofa. In the first place, he could rearrange the little room so its absence would hardly show. In the second, the dolls' house was only one of four of Inez's, and she was already bored with it. The question was purely of the chances of detection, for there was no comparison between Inez's and Philip's need. In Tony's mind theft was associated exclusively with money. Taking things came under the lesser head of "swiping," a form of misdemeanor about which grown-ups could be expected to carry on but which enjoyed much less opprobrium among his contemporaries. There were gradations, of course, even in swiping. One did not take another boy's watch or his camera or (assuming this were possible) his bicycle. But a useless bit of dolls' furniture owned by a spoiled girl who did not even care about it . . . well, only a prude would carp about that. Besides, he would not be taking it for himself.

The theft, or purloinment, or simple swiping,

was accomplished as easily as Tony had foreseen, and Inez was quite unconscious of her loss. The episode filled him with elation. He might have been a prince of olden days who finds himself endowed with the power to heal by touch, or, more appropriately, a Robin Hood whose destiny is to redress, in his own particular fashion, the injustices of contemporary society. He had taken a trump from Inez's hand to provide a better balance in Philip's.

When Susan, their older sister, who was always peering into Philip's dolls' house and making mean remarks about it, saw the divan, she recognized it at once as Inez's.

"You swiped it from her!" she accused Philip.

"I did not! Tony gave it to me."

Susan turned in surprise to Tony. Inez might well have given a present to her handsome brother, but why a doll's divan? "Inez has a funny way of showing her partiality."

"Not at all," Tony retorted. "I told her I wanted it for Philip."

As an answer it seemed to fit, but Tony knew that Susan would make a point of checking his story with Inez. For there was a grown-up quality in Susan. She could always be counted on to do the obvious thing and hence to catch people. Yet he had no sense of alarm, or even of apprehension. The game was becoming exciting.

"Well, I'll ask her next time to give you something for me," Susan said.

And she did this, the very next Sunday, when Inez and her father came to lunch. Inez looked blank.

"You remember, Inez," Tony said coolly. "The little divan from your dolls' house you gave me for

Philip's? I asked you for it as a Valentine's Day present."

Inez looked so bewildered that Tony felt embarrassed for her obtuseness. Then her features seemed suddenly to jump in recognition.

"Oh, the little sofa, of course!" she cried. "Naturally, I gave it to you! It was for Philip, that's right. Do you like it, Philip? Does it fit your room? You must show it to me after lunch."

But after lunch Tony had to walk home with Inez, and when her father had gone upstairs for his nap, he had to kiss her many times in the conservatory. For years afterward ferns would be associated in his mind with wet, thick lips, with the scent of gum drops, with perspiration. He had learned about crime. Now he learned about punishment.

It was not necessary, however, to be caught. Only fools were caught. It was going to take more than Inez's giggles and squirms to make him give up this brave new weapon. A week later he took a miniature piano from the apartment of a friend whom neither Susan nor Philip knew and warned Philip not to show it off to guests. Then he took a book from the library of a friend's father for Susan (he told her it had been a present) and a china ashtray for his mother (he told her he had bought it with his saved allowance). At last he decided that it was time to do something for himself, and he took a yellow fountain pen from a department store counter. This last somehow struck him as a final commitment.

He now found himself in the habit of accumulating small objects at the rate of one a week: figurines, vases, beads, tiny toys, spoons—the world seemed replete with useless, decorative, unmissed chattels. He kept them in the back of his closet and in the bottom of the grandfather clock in the front hall that had never worked. Just why he was turning himself into such a magpie remained a mystery. At times he thought that he must like the feeling that he was doing things, rather than having things done to him. At others he felt that there might be an element of daring in these acts, a kind of challenge to the capricious deity that had made his family's life seem such a dreary one. But all he could be sure of was that he felt a bigger, braver being when his fingers surreptitiously closed around a coveted object.

There might have been a lesson taught by the fact that when detection came, it came after a gross risk quite unnecessarily and uncharacteristically taken. It was on the Lowders' annual summer visit to Grandpa Daly in the big white house in Larchmont. Tony hated this visit. He hated the airs of superiority of the Daly cousins and the bray of the big Irish gathering. He hated his mother's enthusiasm and his father's discomfort. But above all he hated Grandpa Daly.

Grandpa Daly was a small, wiry widower with thick long hair, still brown at eighty, that fell over his forehead in the manner of Will Rogers. But there was little benignity in the sharp-nosed, thin-lipped brown face under that tumbling lock or in the discourse that flowed so relentlessly from that gnarled throat. Tony had never known a human being to talk as much as Grandpa Daly. He seemed to be engaged in a kind of permanent, oral autobiography, a monument of words to the glory of Patrick Daly, varied only by individual paragraphs directed at particular members of his listening family to show them how best to derive profit from his example. Ordinarily, at least at Larchmont, the respectful silence of his descendants was broken only by appropriate laughs or exclamations of assent, but occasionally a querulous grandchild or bibulous son-in-law might attempt a longer interruption or even take the floor, in which event the ancestral voice would rise in pitch and by the exact number of decibels needed to dominate the rival sound, immediately dropping to its former level when the latter was quelled.

It was noted by all, however, that if little knowledge of his relatives could have come in by his ears, enough must have entered through his wandering, shrewd little eyes, for he seemed entirely up to date with the collective and individual failings of his clan. He also seemed to have antennae that picked up the least failure of reverence, for he showed an overt hostility to Tony and directed some of his sharpest comments in the boy's direction. Tony's indifferent marks at school, Tony's preoccupying love of sports, Tony's espousal of the causes of delinquent servants, all came in for grandpaternal comminations. Even at fourteen Tony could sense insecurity in the tyrant who could not endure the smallest sign of independence in his court.

Sometimes at table, the sage of County Cork would pare his fingernails with a tiny scissors that could be pulled out of the interior of a mother-of-pearl pocket knife. This knife intrigued Tony. It was the symbol of his grandfather's immunity from the law that governed others. For anyone else to have pared his nails at table would have been unthinkable. Grandpa himself would have been the first to pounce on him. He was like Louis XIV, who had the lonely privilege of defecating in public. One morning when Tony passed the open doorway of his grandfather's empty bedroom, he spied the knife on the bureau, and, almost before he knew what he was doing, he had entered quickly and seized it. But as he returned to the doorway, he confronted his grandfather coming in. Never was he to forget the expression on that brown, cunning face. It was delight!

"What are you doing in my room, Tony Lowder? What have you got there in your hand? Open your hand at once, sir! At once, I tell you, or I'll call the police! By God, Tony Lowder, if you don't open your hand this second . . ."

Tony dropped the knife and fled.

All morning he waited for retribution. He speculated that his grandfather would select the high publicity of the noontime meal, and he was right. When all were at table, Daly produced his ivory knife and placed it solemnly on the table before him.

"It is my sorry duty, ladies and gentlemen, to have to tell you that our kinsman, Tony Lowder, is a thief!"

Tony's mother gave a cry of alarm; there were gasps of dismay, but Daly raised his arms in the air.

"I caught him red-handed this very morning! Leaving my room with this valuable instrument clutched in his grasping fist! Deny it if you can, Tony Lowder!"

Tony was silent.

"Of course, he can't," the old man continued. "Any more than I, alack the day, can deny he's my own flesh and blood. When I was a boy, in Ireland, my grandfather told me that he could remember the day when a lad was hanged in Galway for the theft of a silver pitcher. It's not my opinion that we have altogether gained from the leniency that has taken the place of the old values."

Daly discoursed throughout the meal on the nefariousness of Tony's crime. There were no interruptions except for Dorothy's occasional gentle sobbing. But Tony knew that this was a necessary demonstration put on for her father's benefit. He found that he fiercely welcomed the break between himself and the old man. There was an end of the hypocrisy of blood love or even blood civility. In the cleaner, airier world that was opening up around him, Patrick Daly, if still a god, was a superseded god. He could rule the Dalys, but he no longer ruled Tony Lowder. The latter was as free and lofty as a Roman citizen who allows a temple in his forum to be dedicated to Jehovah as a gesture of tolerance to an unreasonable little nation that his legions have subdued.

When the meal was over, and the Daly cousins had trooped out of the dining room without speaking to him, Tony went out to the lawn alone. He could not quite analyze his bursting emotion, but he wondered if it might not be happiness.

••

Later that afternoon his real retribution fell, in a totally unexpected way. His father took him up to his room, closed the door and asked him gravely if his grandfather's accusation was true.

"But I admitted it!" Tony exclaimed in surprise.

"You weren't just borrowing the knife, to use it for something?"

"Oh, no."

"You really meant to keep it?"

"Certainly."

"And never return it?"

"Never."

And then, to Tony's horror, George Lowder burst into tears. Never could the boy have imagined that this smiling, taciturn, indifferent parent could have crumpled so completely. It was appalling to discover that a man who had always been so incapable of heights should not be immune to depths.

"Please, Dad." He placed a timid hand on his father's shaking shoulder. "Please, Dad, I can't bear it."

"What's there for you to bear?" George spoke in sudden petulance, as if no blood relationship now existed between them. "You're perfectly self-sufficient. You steal when you want, lie when you want, take everything out of life you want. You're a Daly through and through, despite your grandfather's ranting. He's secretly delighted, of course. Not because you're a thief, but because *I* always rated you above the Dalys. Oh, I never said it. I didn't have to. He knew I thought it, the old devil. He knew from the beginning. And he hates me for it. It's not enough that he and your mother have sucked the blood out of me. They had to take my children, too. Make them pure Daly, so I didn't even have stud value. Well, I never had much hope for Susan or Philip, but I had some for you. And now that's gone."

Tony's eyes, too, were filled with tears. The world in his mind stretched out to an infinite plane of scorched grass. There seemed no end to desolation. "Why didn't you tell me, Dad?"

George seemed surprised at the agony in his tone. "Tell you what?"

"Tell me you believed in me. Tell me what was at stake."

"Oh, Tony, when did any of you ever listen to me?"

"I did. I wanted to, anyway."

George's surprise turned to distrust. He was retentive of grievances. "Well, even if you would have, it's too late now. What's done is done."

"But I don't have to stay a thief."

"Would you swear to stop?" George looked at him doubtfully. "On your word of honor? If you have one?"

"Of course, I will."

George shook his head. "Your grandfather will never believe it. He'll always suspect you."

"Well, who cares about Grandpa? You and I will believe it. Oh, Dad, you'll see. I'll be all the things you want."

The blankness on George Lowder's face might have been something like shame, as if he had conceived a sudden suspicion of what had been sacrificed in his private war with Patrick Daly. But if he had built his life on hate, could it be suddenly switched to love? "Please, Dad," Tony cried in a sudden passion of sincerity. "Please."

"Then tell me. Have you stolen any other things?"

"No."

"This was your first time?"

"My very first."

"Then maybe it's not too late."

Tony hugged his father, and when the latter had

left, he immediately sat down to draw up a list of the stolen objects that had now to be returned. For it was at once perfectly clear to him that thus and only thus could he even hope to convert his egregious lie into a necessary truth.

The weeks that followed the Lowders' return to the city were full ones for Tony. Each stolen chattel had to be the subject of a separate campaign. Some of the campaigns were simple enough. The toys that had been taken from the homes of friends could be easily and secretly restored. But the ornaments and bric-a-brac taken from the homes of grown-ups proved much harder. He had to wait until his mother proposed a visit to the owner and then persuade her to take him along. In one case he had to pretend an interest in a thirteen-year-old daughter of the house that he was far from feeling, which resulted in more sticky kisses in the library while their mothers gossiped in the parlor. Yet there was ecstasy in the moment when he dropped a silver ashtray, shaped like a heart, on the table from which it had been ravished, just as his precocious little hostess slid her impertinent and unwelcome tongue between his lips.

His mother had quarreled with a Daly aunt who had been particularly nasty about the episode of Grandpa's scissors-knife, and Tony was beginning to despair about ever being able to return the ivory seal that belonged with the hunting eskimo on her mantelpiece. His despair was real, for he had got it firmly into his head that a single failure would be enough to invalidate his redemption and to leave him enmeshed forever in the dirty net of his lie. One Sunday morning, however, after a night when he had prayed very hard to a deity whom he was beginning to conceive of as an entity distinct from Grandpa Daly, an entity no longer necessarily disassociated from sympathy, the Daly aunt, Genevieve, called at the apartment after church to make up with her sister. In the flush of their reconciliation Dorothy gave her an azalea plant and Tony, leaping to his feet as he recognized the miracle, cried out to Aunt Genevieve that he would carry it home for her. When he got to her apartment she could not fail to offer him a glass of orangeade, and while she was in her pantry, he restored the little seal to its still empty place. As he did so he saw his glittering eyes in the mirror over the mantel and made the sign of the cross on his chest.

Finally there was only a single trinket left to restore: a tiny doll's flower vase, with yellow and purple latitudinal lines. He had filched it from a notions store while the proprietor and his mother had been discussing the deterioration of the neighborhood, and he had left it to the last because he had thought it would be the easiest to put back. But when he went to the store, he stared in dismay at a show window filled with shiny plumbing fixtures. The notions shop had gone out of business, and inquiry within revealed that the proprietor was dead.

Tony turned back toward home in dazed, solid misery and walked several blocks before he realized that the funny little throb that seemed to be accelerating in his chest was anger. Somebody was making fun of him, somebody even meaner than Grandpa Daly! And taking the little vase out of his pocket, he hurled it on the pavement and ground it under his heel, turning around and around until, looking down, he could distinguish none of the particles. If God would not free him, he would free himself!

But as he resumed his walk, he was conscious of a curious feeling of emptiness. He felt very light, as if with each step he might rise several feet in the air, so that his shoes and clothes acted as weights to keep him down. And then, suddenly, he realized that his anger was quite gone. He stopped again, as if waiting for nature to fill the vacuum, and, surely enough, something seemed to be being pumped into him. His body and mind, his very soul, appeared to be taking the joint shape of a tank, of some kind of receptacle anyway, into which a soft, warm foaming liquid was rapidly flowing. He stood very still in fear of losing the illusion which grew more and more agreeable as his realization of it intensified. Now he was almost flooded to the brim with a sense of unutterable ecstasy, yet the fuller he was, the lighter he became. He might have been a balloon that would float straight up to heaven! He cried aloud in his joy. What could it be but the promised redemption? What could he do but run home, as fast as he could, and fall on his knees to thank God?

Part II

1

Tony had rather taken it for granted that payment by the underworld would be quick and efficient. He had vaguely pictured Max, on a park bench at lunch hour, being joined by a man in dark glasses. No greeting would pass between them, but when the man rose, an envelope with crisp new bills in the exact amount would be left at Max's side. He had to be indoctrinated into the elaborate and clumsy ritual of crime.

"Have our margin gaps been covered?" he asked confidently, when he and Max next met for lunch.

"They've been covered to the extent of eight thousand bucks."

"*Eight* thousand! What happened to the other thirty-two?"

Max glanced evasively about at the neighboring tables. "The first payment was only to be for fifteen."

"Then where's the other seven?"

"Look, Tony, can't you leave that to me? These guys are tricky to deal with."

"So I'm beginning to see."

"All I ask is that you take care of your side. That should be simple enough."

"Not as simple as you so lightly assume. The Regional Director has already asked me what I'm doing in the *Menzies* case."

"No kidding?"

"None whatsoever, I assure you. In his own very special brand of bureaucratise he managed to convey the distinct suggestion that I get off my ass."

"Jesus."

"Precisely. Jesus. I have plenty of little tricks up my sleeve as to how I can stall him, but in the meantime I expect to be compensated. And compensated according to the precise terms of our agreement. So I repeat: where is the other seven?"

"I don't know."

"Come, Max."

Max looked at him now with a desperate, sullen defiance. "Lassatta says he has to pay someone called Rubin. He says it was understood from the start that Rubin's share was to come out of ours."

"And who the hell is Rubin?"

"I don't know exactly. Somebody in Lassatta's union who originally brought him to Menzies."

"But why does he get paid out of *our* share? And for doing what?"

"I guess because he always does."

"Always does what?"

"Always gets a percentage of every Menzies deal."

"Max, you're making no sense. Why should we risk our necks for forty grand and then have it chiseled down by some guy you've never even heard of? Tell Lassatta a deal's a deal. If we don't get every penny of that money, I'm not going to play ball. Menzies, Lippard and Co. can close shop."

"You'd better go easy with that kind of talk. You're playing in a different league now."

Tony stared at his friend with an exasperation that turned to astonishment. For Max's cheeks were as yellow as the table cover. And why, Tony wondered, should fear, simple animal fear, instantly raise such quivering contempt in himself? "Maybe this is what they mean by crime not paying," he observed sarcastically. "And I thought we had figured this out with such masterly precision! The price, you will recall, was the bare minimum that would justify the risk. Even a couple of thousand less, and we would have stayed honest. And now you're talking about cutting it in half."

"I still don't see what else we could have done."

"*Could* have done? You mean you plan to take this lying down?"

"What can I do, Tony?"

"Tell Lassatta what I said. Is it a deal or no deal?"

"You'd better see him yourself."

"I guess I'll have to."

It was finally arranged that Tony and Max and Lassatta should meet in the back of a parked Buick sedan at Broadway and 110th Street on a Saturday afternoon at two. Tony took an immediate dislike to Lassatta, in whose fixed, stale little smile he read the desire to humiliate and bring down to his own level the political candidate.

"Look, Lassatta," he said after some minutes of

pointless discussion. "I'm not pretending to be any bigger or any grander than you or any of your crowd. As far as I'm concerned, we're all crooks together. But if I'm not going to get what I was promised, you're not either. Is that clear? If I get a penny less than forty grand the *Menzies* case goes straight to the Regional Director."

Lassatta's smile became the least bit staler, but his voice was soft. "What about Max's back interest due? Aren't I to take that out?"

"What does that come to?"

"Twelve g's."

Tony turned indignantly to Max. "Is that right?"

"Yeah, that's right." Max was almost inaudible.

Tony brooded for a minute. He knew that Max was too scared to deny it. On the other hand, with so broken an ally, he might do well to settle. "If I concede the interest, Lassatta, will the balance be paid in full? Twenty-eight to the penny? I'm damned if I'll pay this guy Rubin a cent."

"It's the custom, Lowder."

"I don't know anything about customs. I only know the deal I made."

"Take it easy, fella."

"I'll take it as I find it."

"You could make a mistake, you know."

"Two could."

There was a pause, and Lassatta finally shrugged. "Let me talk to Rubin. I'll see what can be done."

"You tell Rubin—and anyone else you want—that the case goes to the Regional Director the first thing Wednesday morning if the whole twenty-eight thousand isn't paid up by midnight Tuesday."

"Say, wait a second, *wait* a second," Lassatta protested, with a note of actual grievance in his tone. "You were to give us two full weeks."

"They expire on Wednesday. And Max and I so far have received a stinking eight thousand bucks. And the Regional Director's on my tail."

Lassatta's eyes dropped. "I told you. I'll see what can be done."

"And I'm telling you I don't care what can be done. If the twenty thousand still due isn't paid up by Tuesday night, I'm through with the *Menzies* case. I don't want to see you again. I don't want to talk about it." He turned to wink at Max with a sudden exhilaration and chuckled at the latter's ashy countenance. "You can call out your gorillas and toss us both in the East River. I couldn't care less. But I promise you, Lassatta, on my sacred word of honor as a neophyte crook, no matter what *you* do, I'll do what I say."

Lassatta looked pained. "It isn't necessary to use that kind of language, Lowder. You're new at this game, and you ought to be willing to learn the rules from those that know."

"I am. But you have to learn mine. What kind of a businessman are you, anyway? Do you think I'd ever do another deal with you, after the way you've treated me in this one?"

Lassatta merely grunted at this, and Tony nudged Max to indicate that the interview was over. He was fairly sure at least of the compromised sum.

At his office, however, on Monday morning, another complication developed. Tod Jennings, the Regional Director, came in to see him. He was one of those very dry, very faithful, very practical public servants, a bit gray, a bit bent, a bit dull, but with unexpectedly sympathetic eyes.

"I thought I'd better check up on the *Menzies* case," he said, almost apologetically. "I've had two more calls about it. There seems to be an impression that they may be in a real jam."

"Is that so?" Tony asked. He puffed at his pipe quietly for a moment as he contemplated his boss. Then he directed his attention to the files heaped up on the right side of his desk. "It must be here somewhere. Let's see. Ah, yes, Menzies, Lippard." He pulled out the file with a little nod of recognition and studied a memorandum clipped to the first page. "There seems to be a question about Lippard's special partnership. It looks a bit complicated. I have a note here to call a Mr. Oxenstern on Wednesday of this week."

"Who's he?"

"Lippard's accountant. He was of the opinion that it could all be cleared up very easily."

"I see. What about our accountant? Have you sent him in yet?"

"No. I thought I'd use Sam Cohn. He was on the Menzies account two years ago. He's had a flare-up of his old ulcer trouble, but he's due in next Monday."

"I think I wouldn't wait for him, Tony. I think I'd put someone else on the job right away."

"Good, sir, I'll do that."

When Jennings had left, Tony decided that he had better be out of the office all Tuesday. He would use the excuse of an annual physical checkup that he had forgotten about and telephone that he would be in early Wednesday. Otherwise Jennings would take the file and reassign it.

Decidedly, things were getting close, but he wondered if he did not prefer it so. Could it be that he needed the feeling that he was earning his money? That he was still a puritan in crime? The idea, anyway, was amusing.

That night was Lee's thirty-ninth birthday, and they celebrated it at home, with a bottle of champagne sent around by her father. Lee claimed that it was the last birthday a woman could recognize, and she told him that she expected him to make passionate love to persuade her that she was still young. He assured her that she would have no complaints, yet when they went to bed, he failed altogether. This had never happened before, except when there had been some obvious reason, like his having drunk too much. In his own bed he lay awake, mortified and discountenanced. Then he heard the scratch of a match. Lee had got up and was smoking on the chaise longue.

"What's wrong?" she demanded in a funny flat tone. "Don't I attract you any more?"

"Oh, come, Lee, you're old enough to know about these things."

"Thanks for reminding me of my age."

"It happens in the best of families. Haven't your girl friends told you?"

"I know all about my girl friends and their impotent husbands. If this was a regular occurrence, I wouldn't give a hoot in hell. But it's not. With you."

"Maybe it will be. From now on."

"What's happened, Tony?"

"Old age."

"Oh, phooey. It's not that. I've lost my appeal for you. Come on. Admit it."

Tony was taken aback by the conviction in that tear-drenched voice. What *had* happened?

"I love you, Lee."

"You beg the question."

"Do you think there's only one way people can show it?"

"I think there's one way *you* can show it."

"What a physical philosophy."

"Isn't it Joan's?"

He thought now that he saw his way out. "Yes."

"Is it because of Joan that you couldn't tonight?"

"Perhaps."

"Because she's dying?"

"Because she's dying.'"

"Is she worse?"

"Yes. I talked to her this afternoon." He wondered if he could even count the lies that he had told that day. "She wants to see me. You needn't worry. She's beyond that kind of thing now."

There was a long silence after this, and he hoped that she had been satisfied. But of course she wasn't.

"Do we have to wait till Joan dies before we make love again?"

"That's a bitchy remark."

"Then I'm a bitch. But I'm still entitled to an answer. *Do* we have to wait?"

"Lee, you're insatiable. Shut up about Joan, can't you?"

"Because she's dying? I don't care if she's dying. Everybody dies. The point is, do any of us live?"

"Very profound."

"What's happening to you, Tony? Don't you care any more about anything?"

For the first time in their marriage he was so angry that he did not mind how much her feelings were hurt. He got up and went to the living room and spent the rest of the night on the sofa. But his sleep was fitful. He had a sensation of being a raft at sea, a raft of loose logs strung together by a rope, except that the rope was gone, and there was nothing to keep the logs from drifting slowly apart, even in still water, without waves or current. It was only a matter of time, and very little time at that, before he would be all over the ocean, before there would be no further visible connection between his individual, rotting pieces of timber.

In the morning he dressed and shaved without talking to Lee, who pretended to be asleep, and breakfasted alone in the kitchen. Then he telephoned his secretary, to say that he would be out all day for a physical examination, and left the apartment to go to Max's office. There, for once, the latter had good news. A representative of Lassatta had delivered an additional eleven thousand dollars.

"There are still nine to go," Tony observed grimly.

"You don't really mean to turn in Menzies if we don't get it?"

"I've never meant anything more. Force is the only language these guys understand."

"Oh, Tony!"

"Leave it to me, Max. You won't get hurt. It's me they'll be after."

Max appeared to derive a desperate hope from this. He had evidently reached a point where he could only close his eyes and rely on the shards of his faith in Tony. "They say we'll get the rest at two o'clock in the men's washroom at Grand Central."

"The men's room? Oh, my prophetic soul! Didn't I tell you?"

"They say you must be there, too."

"I wouldn't miss it for the world."

Tony wondered, at a quarter to two, as he and Max were having their shoes shined in the appointed place, if the underworld did not actually enjoy these clandestine meetings, in parked cars, in back rooms of bars, on park benches. Unlike the business deals with which he had hitherto been associated, the details seemed to be worked out after the agreement had been reached. Perhaps these constant, dark encounters were a kind of diversion, even a form of needed social life. The Mafia must have had a good deal of time on its hands.

Max suddenly rose and followed a pimpled young man in a pinstripe suit into the lavatory. When he returned, alone, he and Tony went up to the main waiting room. Tony sat on a bench, concealing the envelope in his newspaper and quickly counted out four hundred dollars in shabby twenty dollar bills. Then he burst out laughing.

"I deserve it, Max!" he exclaimed. "I deserve the whole damn thing. It's too beautifully ironic! I wanted to be the master of my destiny, and I end up with a small handout in a men's room. Could Samuel Beckett have written it better?"

On their way out of the station Max stopped at a broker's booth and read the ticker. "Don't worry about it too much," he told Tony. "The market's really picking up. I didn't tell you, but Herron was up five points yesterday. If it does the same thing today, we'll get by."

"Ah, but I'm still going to do what I said I'd do!"

"Even if we don't need to?"

"Even so. That will be my dark integrity."

"But Tony, even if we're in the clear?" Max's eyes rolled in entreaty.

"I told you, Max. Leave that side of it to me."

When Tony came home that night he found Lee very cool, but willing to accept a truce. Obviously to her disappointment, he agreed promptly to her suggestion that they should forgo any discussion of the quarrel.

"I have a lot on my mind," he explained. "But I think I'm beginning to see my way out. Give me two more days."

On Wednesday morning, his proposed deadline was past, and Lassatta was still eighty-six hundred dollars short. As soon as he arrived at his office, Tony asked his secretary to make an appointment with the Regional Director.

"As a matter of fact, Mr. Jennings wants to see *you*," she informed him. "When he found that you weren't coming in yesterday, he asked me to send him the Menzies, Lippard file. I suppose it must pertain to that."

Tony, strolling down the corridor to Jennings' office, supposed indeed that it would "pertain" to that. Yet he still found the sense of excitement almost agreeable. Anything was better than those torn, crumpled bills at Grand Central.

Jennings, however, was smiling as he handed the Menzies file back to Tony. "This matter is all arranged," he said. "No further action required. I admit I got a bit hot under the collar when I found you were out yesterday and that nobody else had been assigned to Menzies. But when I'd called for the file and gone over it, I found it was, as you said, all a matter of the terms of Lippard's special partnership. So I telephoned Lionel Menzies, and he told me that we needn't argue the point as he had just obtained further capitalization of four million. I sent somebody over from the accounting department, and this was duly confirmed. So everything's okay. I guess you were right not to get too hot and bothered about it."

"I've had some other dealings with that firm," Tony explained with a dry laugh. "I was reasonably sure they'd be able to meet the requirements. They're pretty sharp cookies."

2

Despite the fact that Tony and Max had received less than half of the original sum offered and only two thirds of the compromised figure, they were able to survive. The market seemed definitely restored, and Max with it. He had lost his haggard look.

"If ever you doubt again the old adage that time is money, remember these terrible days," he told Tony.

"And I suggest that you, too, remember a couple of things," Tony retorted. "Particularly what happens to little boys who fall in with loan sharks. Have you paid off Lassatta yet?"

"Not entirely. I'd have to sell some of our Herron to do that."

"Sell it."

"But, Tony, it's going up. It's bound to go up more!"

Tony contemplated Max's fresh, boyish face with amazement. How was it possible that the fear which had so ravaged him, emotionally and physically, only a week before, should have departed and left no trace? How could a man have been that scared once and take the risk a second time? Was it the saving grace of a superficial man that his fears were superficial, too?

"I should think at this point you might want to play it safe for a bit."

"You mean stop now?" Max demanded. "But we haven't got anywhere yet. You and I haven't taken the risks we've taken just to be a couple of petty bourgeois, I hope."

"You mean you've got another job for me?"

"No, no, no, but I'm certainly not going to sell Herron. Or Alrae. I'm going to hang on to them if it kills me."

"Which I suppose it may. Anyway, so ends our first venture into crime. The only thing I can't understand about it is why it pays Lassatta and Menzies to treat us so foully. Suppose they need to use us again?"

A potential answer to Tony's question seemed to be offered that same evening when a mild, soft-voiced young man accosted him in the street as he walked to the subway.

"Excuse me, Mr. Lowder. I've been sent by Mr. Menzies, Mr. Lionel Menzies. He would like to adjust a certain matter with you. If you would care to come to his apartment now for a drink, he would be very much obliged. I have the car here and can take you."

Tony was amused. The black limousine, the silent drive up the East River, the bar in the car, the use of the back elevator in Lionel Menzies' magnificent apartment building in Sutton Place, all made for a far better scenario than the washrooms and parked cars of his more recent experience. The immense library where his host received him had a baroque stage at one end, framed with twisted columns, on which a dining room table and chairs were set. Between glass cabinets containing golden-backed books reaching to the ceiling were alcoves hung with old paintings and drawings. Tony noticed what he took to be a Van Dyke portrait, a Piranesi print, a Tiepolo drawing. Menzies was a small man, with a round, absolutely bald head and large, beady, laughing eyes. He made Tony think of a bug in an animated cartoon. He talked incessantly.

"I see you like nice things, Mr. Lowder. Are you perhaps a collector yourself? No? But I'm sure you will be. Oh, I can tell. You spotted my Piranesi right off. It really is the best of the prison series. Can't you see it as a set for a Verdi opera? Doesn't it make you want to be a tenor in the last act, discovered by a spotlight in a living tomb and not too starved to sing one last superb aria? Ah, you admire the Tiepolo. That shows you have a real eye. Did anyone ever know skies like Tiepolo? Of course, a drawing is not the thing to see that in, but you must admit he could make a landscape do a minuet. Yes, right under it is a portrait of Corneille. Pierre Corneille who wrote *Le Cid.* We don't believe it was actually done from life, but it's very much of the period, don't you think? Ah, Corneille, who else did more for the *gloire* of France?"

Tony wandered about the chamber, allowing this odd creature to ramble on. Menzies' chatter was self-generated; it needed no response. Was there some necessary connection between crime and banality? Surely it would behoove him to return to the straight and narrow if the lawless were so bound to the cliché. Or was he learning something fundamental about the nature of morality? Could a fine mind exist in the head of a criminal?

"I guess we'd better get down to business, Menzies," he said. "I saved your chestnuts, but I seem not to have got all my own out of the fire."

"My dear young man, you're blunt, and I like bluntness. Let me get you a drink."

The wait seemed interminable. Menzies hovered over a huge bar table, taking stoppers out of decanters, sniffing, measuring drops into spoons, prattling in his prowess in mixtures. But when he finally handed Tony a very small, sweet drink that seemed to have a rum base, his tone changed. He became almost masterful. "I am sorry you were approached by Lassatta. It was entirely unnecessary. Men like you and me, Mr. Lowder, need no intermediaries. I shall be glad to make up to you the balance due, but only on condition that in the future you and I deal exclusively with each other."

"Why should there be a future?"

Menzies blinked his eyes, as if with pleasure at his guest's wit. "You mean why should you go through that again? Of course, you shouldn't. And you shan't. Hear what I propose. I propose to establish an account for you in my firm, under the name of a nominee, of course. You will have the privilege of making withdrawals whenever you wish. I suggest that we start with a balance of whatever it was that Lassatta shortchanged you. What was it?"

"Eighty-six hundred."

"Very well. We'll make it eighty-six hundred. You see, I ask no confirmation, nor do I have any way of checking. I did not even know for certain there *had* been a short change. I simply assumed it, knowing Lassatta. The moment I heard that he was in it, I knew I would have to wait till he had made all his infantile blunders. But I can usually bide my time."

"For what, Mr. Menzies?"

"For our partnership. For our little silent partnership. Our little silent exclusive and very profitable partnership. I am suggesting, Mr. Lowder, that you agree to be discreet and honest with all the world—but me. I suggest that at chosen times and in very carefully chosen places, you and I meet to exhange useful bits of information about corporate secrets and government projects. I am an investor, and an investor needs news. That is all. Not much, is it? But on it we can build empires."

"Empires?"

"Well, empires of Tiepolos, anyway."

"You assume I'm going to stay in government. Suppose I go back to my law practice?"

Menzies shrugged. "Then I've lost my investment. But you won't. You've got politics in your blood now. You'll go far. Besides, you'll have me behind you."

Tony stared, fascinated, at this small, smiling man. "Why should we trust each other?"

"Because it will be so much worth our while." Menzies suddenly clapped his small fat hands. "And because I've studied your record. I believe that this has been your first crime. Am I right?"

"I'm glad you call it a crime, anyway."

"Oh, I know you," Menzies exclaimed eagerly. "With anyone else, I'd have winked and used the word 'peccadillo.' But not with you. Not with Tony

Lowder. You will be both an economist and a realist in crime. You will always know precisely what you are doing, and you will always be sensible enough to do the bare minimum. So long as you have only one Menzies and I only one Lowder, nobody will ever catch us. Nobody will even know we're acquainted."

Tony put down his abominable drink and resumed his roaming of the great room. Never had he felt less a part of the real world. Had it not been for the sugar and grenadine in the cocktail he might have thought he was living in a dream—or in a 1935 movie with Norma Shearer and Clark Gable. Did all great men have a Menzies in their past? And yet what deal could have been more perfectly adapted to his needs? Where, even, was the risk?

"But it must be understood that it's only you and me," Menzies cautioned him. "So far as Lassatta is concerned, you've become disgusted with bribery. He will have driven you back to grace. And your friend Leonard must think the same. I cannot afford to have anything more to do with that jackass. For, you see, Mr. Lowder, I, too, am returning to grace. You and I can't afford the sloppy contacts of the underworld."

Tony came back and stood before him. "If I rejected your offer, Mr. Menzies, I should be making further hash of the hash I've already made of my life. Like Corneille, we must go on for the *gloire.*" Tony now threw back his head and uttered a shout of laughter. It occurred to him in the midst of it that Menzies might understandably take offense. But he didn't. He laughed, too. "Mr. Menzies, I think I may be your man!"

He telephoned Max from a pay booth and told him to meet him downstairs in the lobby of his apartment house. Because Menzies had asked him to exclude Max, he could not even wait until the morning to bring him in. They sat on a marble gray bench in the blank gray corridor, watching the cooperative owners, returning from work, walk hurriedly and sightlessly to their elevators. But Max seemed to find what Tony had to say difficult to follow. He scratched his knee; he scratched his ankle.

"I know I can make it now with what we've got," he assured Tony. "Herron's up another five points today."

"Then we're out of the woods. Because I've got the eighty-six hundred."

Max's eyes glittered. "From Lassatta?"

"Hell, no. We're through with Lassatta. For good and all. From here on we work with Menzies. It's not only safer. It pays. And it pays real money."

"Does Lassatta know?"

"What the hell business is it of Lassatta's?"

"Oh, Tony, suppose he finds out."

"How can he find out? And why should I care if he does? We should never have got mixed up with Lassatta in the first place."

Max grasped Tony's hand so tightly that his nails pierced the skin. All his old desperation had returned. "Let go, damn it!" Tony exclaimed in pain as he tore his hand free. "What's come over you, Max? Have you lost your senses?"

"Tony," Max pleaded. "I've told you before, you don't know the kind of men you're dealing with.

They'll never let you get away with this. Do you think you can use Jerry Lassatta as a ladder to Lionel Menzies and then just kick him over?"

"I didn't use him as a ladder. Menzies approached me directly. The whole idea was Menzies'."

"That doesn't matter. You found out about Menzies through Lassatta. He set the whole thing up. That's the way he does business. And once he's started something he *never* lets go."

"He should have thought of that when he welshed on the deal he made with us. So far as I'm concerned, he has let go."

"Tony, it won't work, I tell you."

"Max, be realistic. What can he do?"

"He can kill us."

Tony contemplated the pinched lips, the lined brow, the blinking eyes of his friend and reflected that he never should have told him. He should simply have arranged that Max share his profits. He tried now to make some of his old feeling come back by placing his arm around Max's shoulder.

"Steady, old pal."

"Oh, Tony, be reasonable!" And Max, shuddering, uttered a little sob. Tony's heart hardened again, and he removed his arm.

"I don't know how long I can live with this terror of yours."

Max leaned forward, his elbows on his knees, and covered his face with his hands. "I don't know how long I can live with it myself," he groaned.

3

On the Saturday after Easter Tony and Lee drove down to the end of Long Island to lunch with the Conways. The sky was so blue and the road so smooth that Tony could not help occasionally bursting into song. Lee was silent.

"If you can't enjoy today, you can't enjoy anything," he reproached her. "It makes one wonder if life was worth living before they invented the automobile."

"The automobile? I thought it was your investments that made you so happy. That stock that sounds like a bird. Herron?"

"Well, of course, I'm glad Herron's going up. And, of course, I'm glad that Horton has submitted my name to the President. I want to be Assistant Secretary of the Treasury. All that is fine. Very fine. But don't you ever feel that happiness can be just a matter of feeling well on a nice day?"

"No. I keep thinking of Joan. Everything seems to be going so right for us, but it's all so wrong for her. So we should be exuberant—as you obviously are. And Joan should be desperate—as I gather she is. And yet I have the funniest feeling that I'm not that much better off than she is."

"You don't mean you feel ill?"

"No. It's just that dying doesn't seem as bad as it used to."

"Oh, Lee, on a day like this!" Tony's sudden burst of exasperation flooded and drowned his sympathy. "What makes you so perverse? Haven't I been doing all the things you wanted? Aren't I less worried about money? Don't I come home earlier? Hasn't Max stopped telephoning at night?"

"Yes. And I've never felt farther away from you."

Tony wondered with a groan if there were any point in scheming to make any woman happy. "You're the most contrary creature I ever imagined. Why do you have to be this way now that I've got everything fixed?"

"Why are you behaving so peculiarly?"

"Peculiarly?"

"You act as if every day might be your last."

"That's a perfectly good way to live, isn't it?"

"But it never used to be yours. Now you act as if you'd been condemned to death, like Joan. Have you?"

"Damn it all, enjoy yourself!" he cried. "That's an order."

Joan's house, appropriately called "Land's End," was placed at the very tip of a stony peninsula that stretched far out to sea on the northern shore of the island. Its single gray story climbed up and down along the rocks with long glass windows that faced the Atlantic. Joan loved to spend winter weekends in it. She would sleep under heavy covers with the whole eastern side of her bedroom opened to the noisy sea. But now it was a benign day, and the Atlantic was calm and white and sparkling under the light blue sky. Joan, in a scarlet shirt and white slacks, looking uncannily healthy and brown, took Tony by the arm as soon as they had appeared on the terrace and led him to a seat directly over the water. Obviously, she had no time for other guests.

"I'm way past politeness, way past," she explained sharply. "Everybody knows and understands, including Lee, so what the hell?"

"But, Joan you're looking so well!"

"It's inside, honey, not out, and it's there all right. Don't worry about *that.* But I may have months yet, and months are beginning to seem like a lot of time to me. Tell me, do you really believe in nothing at all? About God and heaven?"

"Oh, rot, of course I do. I used to say I didn't because people expect you to. It's not fashionable to believe."

"Really? Since when did you care about fashion? But, anyway, what *do* you believe in?"

Tony carefully allowed his smile to fade. "I believe that when you die, you go to heaven and see all the people you love."

"And what do you do there? Play harps?"

"If you want to."

"Forever and ever?"

"Well, for a long time. For as long as you like."

She frowned. "You won't be serious. You're a meatball."

"I am serious."

"Oh, you're serious about wanting to comfort me. You always want to comfort people. But don't you see that all that cant about immortality and harps is even more scary than total extinction? Because in this life at least we have the mystery of death. But suppose there were no mystery? Suppose it were all explained and there you were. Just waiting?"

"Well, then, maybe there is extinction. My point is that whatever it is, it's going to be all right."

"I never heard anything so fatuous. But, of course, you don't believe it. You're just being nice. Everybody is. They comfort me and avoid me, as if I had leprosy. Leprosy! I wish I had."

"Joan." He gripped her hand. "Joan, be quiet. Relax."

"Oh, Tony, it's so hard to get used to." She didn't care that the others, talking louder, talking nervously, could see her tears. "And then the straws I cling to. Melanie Hunt, you know her. She's on the Met board. She told me that they had a miracle at the Cloisters last Sunday. On Easter. Or rather Easter eve, at midnight. They're keeping it quiet because they don't want crowds trooping up. But one of the guards saw the Chalice of Antioch levitate. Actually levitate! It rose in the air three inches and just hovered there! And he called two other guards, who saw it, too." After a pause, she shrugged. "But then, I gather, it settled down and hasn't been up since."

"How is that a straw?"

Joan looked at him with mild surprise. "Well, wouldn't it show that Christ was real or something?"

"Would it?"

"All right, you think it doesn't." She held up her empty glass imperiously to the butler. "And, of course, you're right. They figured out it was some kind of electric effect in the cloth under the chalice. Caused by overheating in the furnace below or some damn thing like that. I don't know. All I can be sure of is that my poor little miracle was no miracle. But do you know what, Tony? I went up to the Cloisters and stood for a whole hour before that bloody chalice. And do you think it had the manners to levitate even once? Even one tiny inch?" Tony shook his head. "You're darn right." She called harshly to the butler. "Where's that drink, damn it?"

Norry Conway, very big and scarlet-faced, with graying hair and haggard eyes, dressed in sport clothes that tried to defy death and cancer, came over to them, holding a small white Tiffany box.

"It's not really an anniversary, darling, but it's a kind of one," he said awkwardly. "According to my diary we closed title to this place exactly nine years ago come Tuesday. Anyway, as long as we have our friends for lunch today . . ."

"And as long as we don't know how much time I may have!" Joan interrupted him in a high, tight voice.

Norry looked down at the terrace and shifted his package from one hand to the other.

"Come, Joan," Tony whispered to her sternly. "You can do better than that. I don't care how sick you are."

"Watch me, then!" she exclaimed. She jumped up to catch the others' attention. "Look, everybody! Norry has brought me an anniversary present. On the anniversary of our buying this land. Just nine years ago. Perhaps we should have waited for the tenth, but Norry has always been precipitous. Let's see my loot!"

She sat down at the round, low mosaic table in the center of the porch, and Norry placed the package before her. Everyone crowded around, and Joan raised the box so all could see. When she opened it, there was a deep general gasp.

It was a huge square diamond, alone, free of ring or pendant, on a tiny black cushion. Tony recognized it at once and saw that the others did. It was the diamond that had been sold the preceding week at Parke-Bernet for six hundred thousand dollars, believed to have been purchased by a famous actress. It seemed to burn on its cushion, and yellow and blue lights started from it. Joan turned the box slowly around and around on the table before the hushed group.

"Oh, Norry," she murmured. "Oh, Norry, you angel."

Suddenly she picked the diamond out of its case and pressed it tightly against her heart, as if it might have x-ray powers that could penetrate her body and reach in deep to destroy the multiplying germs that were destroying her. She made a cup of her hands and held the jewel up to her face, leaning forward over it and rocking to and fro. She uttered a low murmur, like a croon. Tony was startled by the expression in her eyes. They were warm, vibrant, loving. She might have been a newly delivered mother looking at her babe.

"Oh, Norry, I love it!" she whispered hoarsely. "Norry, I adore it!"

In the atmosphere of general constraint Norry turned with relief to the white-coated figure of the butler appearing in the doorway. "Oh, is lunch ready, Len? Good, I think we can all use some."

••

The dining room walls were painted green and blue to create undersea atmosphere, and the only paintings, brilliantly lit, were the Odile Redons, of strange, jewel-like marine monsters. Tony was seated on Joan's right, but she had placed her diamond before her, and she would not talk. But as he sat there silently, sipping his white wine, he experienced something that put conversation out of the question.

At first, he had a sense of the sky darkening outside as if the sun had been clouded over. Yet he was facing the long, curved bay window that looked on the sea, and it was perfectly apparent that no clouds had diminished the brilliant sunlight that fell on the sparkling water. The darkness, which made him think of a scrim over a stage set, must have been a thing of his imagination, yet even when he closed his eyes and shook his head, he could not rid himself of this impression of darkness, right there, all over the room, permeating the harsh light, so that black and white seemed to coexist in a queer blend of blindness and vision.

After some minutes, as the vision continued, he began to peer cautiously about the room at the objects and people. The Redon paintings, which he had always before admired, now seemed unaccountably dreary. They might have been executed by a commercial artist on the order of a department store. The beautiful Lowestoft that covered the table, blue and white, struck him as showy and pretentious, and the friends, all chatting about themselves, however lively and well-dressed, seemed the most ordinary of mortals. And yet even here his old sense of observation had not wholly deserted him, for he still could see that the Lowestoft was of a rare quality and he recognized that at least one of the guests was a near great poet. What was the meaning of the two levels of observation? What was *he*?

He! Maybe that was it. As he saw himself, there were not—this was suddenly clear—two levels. He was sure of one thing only. He was the man to whom the room *looked* the new way. He was the man to whom the universe was now surpassingly dull. It would be his punishment to live in this dull universe. Punishment for what? His crime? Was he experiencing the old horror of solitary guilt in the presence of persons not guilty? Was he being swept with the despair of a damned soul who sees the elect in Paradise and knows that he can never join them, a despair intensified by the very failure of the elect to realize his excluded status and the cruel mockery of their continuing to regard him as one of themselves? But no, it wasn't this. It was something much worse. They were not in Paradise and never would be. Paradise had disappeared. He had hurled himself out of it and had fallen into a strange limbo where he existed alone. The people who surrounded him—even Lee, yes even Lee—were not really people any longer. They were the ghosts of the people he had known in Paradise and, like all ghosts, they existed without pleasure or taste. Without companionship. And there was no seeming end to it.

And finally, as if these realizations were only the whistling, stiffening breezes that immediately precede a storm, came the sudden inundation, through his mind and body simultaneously, of a misery, the intensity of which he had never even conceived. He held himself rigidly still, in the horrid apprehension that the least movement might make the pain worse, might make it unbearable so that he would scream and rush from the table.

"What's wrong with you? Are you sick?"

Tony turned to look at Joan. Her face seemed strange and white. She might have been a visitor, in a hospital, looking down on him in a bed.

"I suddenly realized I'm damned."

She continued to stare. "You look absolutely green. Would you like to go and lie down?"

"No, no, it's mental."

"You mean, like a depression?"

"I guess so. A fit of depression. Except I wonder if it will pass."

"Tony! You're acting so strange."

"I'm feeling so strange. I've done a wicked, criminal thing, and I disgust myself."

Joan looked down at her diamond for a moment and then covered it over with her hand. "What kind of a criminal thing?"

"It doesn't matter. It's done."

"Will there be consequences?"

"There have been. That's what I'm telling you."

"No. I mean real consequences. Like the police or something."

"What does it matter?" He was suddenly impatient with her silly questions. "If I told you I were going to suffer some horrible, old-fashioned punishment, like being broken on the wheel, I wouldn't care."

"Or like dying of cancer?" Joan had finally remembered herself.

"That's right. I envy you, Joan."

The fact that he did not care enough about convincing her to put the least conviction in his tone did the job better than any emphasis. "I believe you do," she murmured in awe. "But then you're very brave. That's why I envy *you*. Why I've always envied you."

"Brave?" He snorted. "What's bravery?"

"Not being afraid of pain. Or dying."

"It depends what the pain is. I'm afraid of what's inside me now. If I could run away from it, you'd see how brave I was." He clenched his fist in a sudden spasm of misery. "I'd put on a skirt and fight my way into a lifeboat ahead of any number of women and children."

Joan abandoned her diamond and reached under the table to touch his hand. But when she felt the tremor of his clenched fist, she withdrew. "You poor darling, I believe you would. What *has* happened? Is it bad conscience?"

"How do labels help?"

"Maybe you could pray."

"Do you?"

"Oh, yes. Constantly. When I'm not abusing God, I pray to him."

"You think this is a religious experience I'm having?"

"Couldn't it be?"

"You and your chalice. It could be anything. Except I don't feel repentant. I only feel damned. Can you be damned if there's no God and no heaven? It's a paradox, but I can believe it."

"Couldn't you make some kind of restitution? They say you can't buy back innocence, but I wonder if that's true. If you've hurt somebody, you can pay damages. If you've embezzled, you can put the money back. There's not much you can do about murder, but I suppose you haven't gone *that* far."

"Where would I get the money?"

"From me, of course. What do I need money for?"

"You know I can't touch your money."

"Is that sensible? If you're damned and I'm dying?"

"It isn't sensible. But there's very little that's happening to me that makes any sense." Again he shivered with impatience. "All I know is that I wish I were dead."

Joan almost smiled. It was the nearest thing to a smile anyway in their curious interchange. "It would be cozy if you went with me. I'd mind everything much less. But whatever it is, you'll get over it. You're so strong, lover. You're the strongest man I've ever known. And I wish I'd married you. I think we'd have got on."

"You'd have hated being poor."

When he had said this, he did not want to go on with the conversation. Joan would never understand what had happened to him, and what good could it do him if she did? Tactfully, she turned to her other neighbor, and he was left to silence as the woman on his right had given him up as hopeless. He had a fierce urge to leave the dining room, to go down to the rocks and to run by the sea, run as hard as he could. He was just about to excuse himself when Joan rose, and the terrible meal was over.

On the long drive home he answered Lee in abrupt monosyllables. Her questions about the party irritated him furiously. Never could he recall having been so unreasonably angry. But the pain was actually growing. He had to concentrate on the road to keep the car from swerving.

"You seemed to have had plenty to say to Joan at lunch," Lee observed tartly. "Is that why you're all talked out?"

"Yes."

"Well, you don't have to bite my head off."

"Lee, will you try to understand something? I think I'm starting a nervous crack-up. I have the most terrible sunk feeling. Like a migraine."

"You mean you have a headache?"

"Much worse. Much!"

"Oh, Tony, what *is* it?"

The tense anxiety in her tone only infuriated him. "Oh, leave me be, will you? I'll come out of it. Just leave me be."

"Well, it makes a girl feel just great to be told to shut up by a husband who's been shooting his mouth off all day to another woman."

"Joan's different. She's dying."

"Is that the only way to your wounded heart? Rather a stiff price to pay, don't you think? Do you mind if I wait until the children are a little older?"

"What a handy thing jealousy is!" Tony almost shouted. "It exempts you from the least chore of sympathy. All you have to do is imagine that I'm paying attention to another woman, and I can suffer the tortures of hell for all you care!"

Lee was silent, and for some minutes he drove on without even glancing at her. Then he heard her stifled sobbing and knew that he had really hurt her. For Lee was no easy weeper. Always in the past her tears had been a terror to him, and few indeed had been the concessions that he would not allow to make them cease. But now everything was different. Her resentment seemed to him unreal, egocentric, not really concerned with him. He would not apologize or attempt to console her. Grimly he gripped the top of the wheel and stared down the middle of the road. When he stopped at their apartment house Lee got out, dry-eyed, without a word. As he drove about to look for a parking space, he knew that their breach was grave.

4

Tony had met both Joan and Lee in the winter of 1954. He always looked back on that year as the dividing point of his life, a period of brief but heady independence between his final resolution to give up fussing about his parents and siblings and his acquisition of new and more permanent subjects for emotional untidiness.

He was twenty-seven. He had the Korean War behind him and a silver star for bravery as a rocket ship skipper in the Inchon landings. He had almost forgotten the religious flutterings of adolescence. He had learned to leave his prickly relatives to their chosen injustices and to live for Tony Lowder.

He found his lawyer's duties in Hale & Cartwright congenial to his post-combat nature. He loved being able to throw all his force into a given case, without having to fret unduly over the equities. He had been allowed to cut his legal teeth on a cluster of small law suits, the kind that big firms have to take on as accommodations: divorces of relatives of partners, claims by discharged domestics, nuisance suits amounting to petty blackmail. The clients were pleased by his vigorous representation, and Tony received good raises. It struck him that the typical customer of Hale & Cartwright wanted his lawyer to be a bulldog that licked his hand and snarled at everyone else.

Tony did not kid himself, when he defended a rich woman, notoriously forgetful, against the claim of a small milliners' shop which she swore she had never patronized, or contested the suit for alimony of a penniless wife against a husband who was currently bankrupt but the heir to future millions, that he was serving any great cause or promoting any public good. But people had to have lawyers, didn't they? And Tony Lowder had to make a living.

Max Leonard was the self-appointed politician among the clerks of Hale & Cartwright, the man who studied the backgrounds and habits of the partners to try to determine what sort of associate they were most likely to promote, the man who was always gossiping with other associates about their chances, the man who considered every possible way of "making the grade" but the obvious one of hard work. Yet he had a charm to cover his buzzing activity and an ingenuity to conceal his basic superficiality. Tony saw through Max, but he found him pleasant, largely because Max so much admired him. The latter was already probing the possibilities of their setting up on their own, and Tony suspected that Max, if on the light side for Hale & Cartwright, might still be the perfect front man for a smaller organization.

It was at the Leonards' apartment that he first

met Joan. Elaine Leonard, whose blonde prettiness already augured a plump figure and who was already expressing public doubts that she and Max were the perfect young American couple they had seemed at their wedding, was torn between her jealousy of Max's constant fussing over his handsome friend and her own pleasure at having Tony around.

"Who is that stunning girl in the corner?" Tony asked her. "She looks like the heroine of a Joan Crawford film. You know the type: cool, possessed, ambitious."

Elaine did not need to turn around. "It's Joan Lane, not Joan Crawford. But at the end of the movie you'll find she's just the same. She won't, like a Crawford heroine, have given up everything for love."

"Let me be the judge of that."

"You want to meet her? Don't get too thick. Max has other plans for you. He wants you to marry an heiress."

"Must we do everything Max says?"

"You'll find it's easier. It saves you from being manipulated with hidden wires."

"Why didn't *he* make a rich marriage?"

"He should have. But never fear. He'll live again in you. Perhaps he and I both will."

"What kind of talk is that?"

Elaine's eyes rested on him, mocking, irked, even rather desperately hopeful. "Does it embarrass you, Tony, to have made a hit with both the Leonards?"

But Tony had grown too accustomed to Elaine to be embarrassed by her. "Do me a favor, will you? Introduce me to Joan."

When he had taken the other man's place in the

corner with the tall, pale girl with the long black hair, he felt at first that she might not have noticed the substitution. She had been talking about decorating, which was evidently her trade, and she continued to discuss a sample of new material which Elaine had pinned to the curtain behind them.

"But then I suppose the room's such a medley it doesn't matter," she concluded.

"You don't like the room?" Tony asked.

"I didn't say that, Mr. Lowder. But actually I don't. However, it's not important. This is the way all our friends live till the second baby. Then they move to the suburbs and life becomes serious. The first apartment is for making love and storing wedding presents."

He had been right, after all, about the Joan Crawford movie. "And will you start the same way?"

"Oh, I want to start much better. Or stay where I am. Are you ambitious, Mr. Lowder?"

"Tony."

"Are you ambitious, Tony?"

"I've never been able to decide."

"Then you're not."

"Should I be?"

Joan shook her head, as if the question were not worth answering. Her gravity was becoming to her long face and dark, defensive eyes. "Max is always talking about you. Now Max is ambitious. Maybe he thinks he has enough ambition for both of you."

Tony thought already that he was going to like her. "You haven't told me what your ambition is."

"I didn't say I had one."

"You said you wanted to start better than the

Leonards. Or is ambition only concerned with ends? It's not as apt to be concerned with means."

He saw by the automatic quality of her smile that although she recognized humor, she did not much relish it. Smiling with her was probably a matter of manners. "My ambition is concerned with things. Beautiful things. I want to travel and see them. I want to own them. Some of them, anyway."

"You mean, like paintings, sculptures?"

"Yes. And furniture. Porcelains. Jewels. I'm very serious about jewelry."

Tony noted that she wore none but a small sapphire ring. "So you must marry a rich man."

"I guess that's about it. I must marry a rich man. Or remain an old maid with my dreams."

"I'm not a rich man."

"Oh, I know that."

"Even if I became a successful lawyer, I shouldn't be rich enough to buy the things you want. For I imagine they're great things. Rembrandts and such."

"I suppose they are."

"So where does that leave us?"

Her smile was suddenly charming, because they were not being funny. "As friends," she replied. "A little-explored but not unsatisfactory relationship."

After some twenty minutes of this kind of talk, she agreed to have dinner with him. At the restaurant they had further drinks and then, almost without other preliminaries, they exchanged life stories. Only after they had finished dinner did their congeniality strike them as rare.

"Of course, I was prepared for you," she confessed as she took a sip of brandy. "I was intrigued by what Max told me about you. I put you together as a person with whom one could be honest, but I had no idea how honest. It's extraordinary. I've never admitted to anyone the things I've admitted tonight. Why do you suppose that is?"

"Because I'm the unshockable man."

"I can see why I need the unshockable man. But what on earth have you to get out of me?"

"Leave that to me."

She gave him a level look. "I suppose you think you can sleep with me."

"Is it so impossible?"

"Definitely."

"We can leave that to the future. If I ever suggest it, it will be because you want it."

Joan closed her lips tightly. She seemed for a moment to have lost her breath. "I want it now, don't you know that? But if you think I do all the things I want to do, you don't begin to know me."

"I'm beginning to know you. And now, if you've finished that brandy, I'll take you home. I have to be in court at nine tomorrow."

And so their strange friendship began. They went out together every two weeks, and on alternate dates Tony even allowed her to pay. Never once did he make a pass at her. She had told him all he needed to know, and he would recognize the moment–if it came. If it did not, well, New York was full of girls.

She told him about Norris Conway, whom Tony had also met at the Leonards'. He was handsome in a way that was blond and beefy, agreeable in a way that tried too hard not to condescend, conscientious in a way that feared to be brutal. Norris was determined to win every medal in life on his own, or at least to look as if he had. He was probably better off being rich, for without the modern compulsion of the wealthy not to seem proud, he might have been very arrogant indeed. He had the heir's fear of being "done," and to be married for his money would have been to be done in the worst way of all.

"My trouble is that everyone's on to me," Joan protested to Tony. "God knows why, for I never talk. I guess I must smell of it."

"You look deep, that's your trouble. And you are deep. People think deep people have hidden motives. And they do."

"I could have brought Norry around months ago if I had even half a million of my own. Why the very rich think the merely rich won't marry them for their money, I can't imagine. Norry's smitten, all right, and I'd make him a splendid wife. But he's got his ear back like a scared horse."

"Maybe I can help."

"How?"

"A little jealousy might do the trick."

"But he doesn't know anything about you and me."

"Now."

Joan said nothing more that night, but he perfectly understood that she had not liked the suggestion.

He also understood that she did not like the conviviality that had sprung up between him and her parents. Joan was fiercely protective about the old people and did not want her friends to sneer at them. On the other hand, she seemed to fear some possible exposure of herself in Tony's obvious admiration of her mother. Mrs. Lane was Joan's slave, but flattered by a young man, who could tell what disloyalty she might not be capable of?

Mr. Lane was a cheerful nonentity, both to the world and to his family—a coughing, stuttering, stertorous, red-faced old man, a neat, clean bundle of aimless hospitality, not unlike Tony's own father. Mrs. Lane had the more vivid personality. She was round and dumpy, but her dyed black hair and bangs, her many false jewels and tassels, her long, thin nose, her large blinking eyes and hoarse voice, had a dowdy distinction, like that of a retired English actress trying to impress the boarding house with memories of her Imogene or Portia. And, indeed, as Tony discovered, there was some basis for the comparison, for Mrs. Lane as a girl had shown a flair for the stage and had studied in Paris and even been praised by the great Bernhardt, before her father, a professor of religion, had hurried her back from the prospect of a life of sin to the safer arms of Jacob Lane.

"You must recite something to me," Tony urged her one evening at the Lanes' tiny apartment, as jammed and eclectic as a Third Avenue antique shop. "What is the great scene from *Phèdre*? The one all the French school children have to learn?"

"Now, Tony," Joan protested, "if you start Mother on *Phèdre*, we'll be here all night."

"Well, let's be here all night. How about it, Mrs. Lane?"

"I don't know if I still remember any of it," Joan's mother murmured deprecatingly, glancing at the husband who never failed her.

"Come, Jenny, give Tony a few verses. You know you can."

As Mrs. Lane looked down at the plush seat of

the sofa and fingered an unpholstered button, it was evident that she was going to recite and that her mere intention to do so had instantly increased her status in that small chamber. Even Joan was now respectfully silent. Mrs. Lane's long-slumbering muse might have been a kind of Aladdin's lamp which, when rubbed, had still the power to subdue her family to an admiring vigil. Then she began to speak, and her voice was sharp, almost rasping, but very tense and very articulate. The French words seemed to emanate from another woman altogether:

> *"Ah, cruelle, tu m'as trop entendue!*
> *Je t'en ai dit assez pour te tirer d'erreur.*
> *Eh, bien, connais donc Phèdre et toute sa fureur.*
> *J'aime."*

It was astonishing to see what dignity, what depth were conveyed to the bland old wrinkled face by Mrs. Lane's art. The dumpy figure seemed to elongate, to throw off its frills and badges, to suggest that behind the frame, perhaps behind the frame of every woman, lurked the ravaged soul of Theseus' queen. Tony recalled a novel, read in college, where the heroine, a rising young actress, scornfully rejects the proposal of a rising young diplomat conditioned on her giving up the stage. For how could she compare being an admirable ambassadress to being an admirable Phèdre? Surely, Mrs. Lane had made the wrong choice, for she had become nothing, produced nothing. Except Joan. Except Joan—precisely. Maybe Joan was the justification of her sacrifice. For Joan *would* be a great ambassadress.

"You should still go on the stage, Mrs. Lane!" he cried when she had finished. "Think what you have to teach us!" He turned to Joan. "Do you think anyone in our generation could love that way?"

"No, thank God!"

Another extraordinary thing about Mrs. Lane was that she appeared entirely to comprehend Tony's relationship with Joan. One evening, when he came early and found Joan still out, Mrs. Lane sent her husband downstairs to buy a cigar and proceeded to talk frankly to Tony about Norris Conway.

"I'd really rather she married you."

"Just because I like *Phèdre*?"

"Well, that's a kind of reason, isn't it? Norris Conway has never heard of *Phèdre*."

"But why do you assume, Mrs. Lane, that I want to marry Joan?"

"Well, don't you?"

"No. We're not suited at all. Joan's got to be grand. It's her style. It's her trade. She'd be wasted on me, and I on her. Now with you it's different. I feel that you and I understand each other. If anything were to happen to Mr. Lane, which God forbid . . ."

Mrs. Lane gave a little shriek of laughter. "Oh, Tony, promise that if Joan does marry Norris, you'll still come in and see us old folks once in a while."

"Oh, I don't have to promise that. How could I stay away?"

The day after this conversation Tony called Norris Conway and asked him to lunch. They talked of fishing and politics and mutual friends, but afterward, as they paused at the entrance of Norris' office building, Tony asked him casually:

"Tell me, Norry, are you off Joan Lane?"

Norris immediately stiffened. "What do you mean?"

"Just that."

"What's it to you?"

"I'd like to know if the way's clear, that's all. I don't want to waste my time if you've got her sewed up. Are you engaged, or anything like that?"

"I guess that's something you'll have to find out for yourself," Norris said heavily. He was clearly upset.

"Good. I will."

"Well, don't go telling her I insinuated we were engaged." Then he added gruffly: "Anyway, we're not."

Tony now let a month go by without calling Joan. When he finally did so she asked him up for cocktails. Her voice was very cold, and the invitation sounded like an order. He arrived and found her alone. Her parents were south on an "annual sponge," as she put it, with a rich, but distant cousin in Palm Beach.

"I want you to tell me what you did to Norry Conway," she said, when he had mixed his drink. She already had her own, as if she had prepared herself for a scene.

"What makes you think I did anything?"

"Something he said."

"Has he been attentive?"

"Very."

"How gratifying."

"Do you really find it so?"

"I want what you want."

"I see." Joan was very definite now "Then you did speak to him. You did it to make him jealous."

"And I evidently succeeded."

"Oh, yes. It worked like a charm. Except for one thing. You should have gone on taking me out."

"Why?"

"Because your failure to do so, after Norris told you we were *not* engaged, made it look as if you and I were in cahoots."

"So!" Tony exclaimed in surprise. "I never thought of that. Because, of course, we weren't. But it's easily remedied. All I have to do is tell him that he scared me off."

"You needn't. I've already told him."

"That he scared me off?"

"No. That he didn't. I've told him that I *have* been out with you. Twice in the last month."

Tony whistled. "You are a cool one. And it worked?"

"Oh, it worked divinely. He's on the point of proposing."

He raised his glass. "Congratulations, Mrs. Conway!"

Joan looked at him with a countenance from which she had carefully obliterated the least expression. "Is that all you have to say?"

"All *I* have to say! What about you? Aren't you going to thank me?"

"Stop joking, Tony. Just for once." She closed her eyes for a moment.

"I don't propose to be grim about this, you know."

"What *do* you propose?"

"That we be frank. You resent my helping you to marry another man. No matter what we both think is best for you, you have a fixed female resentment against any man who doesn't cast himself at your feet. But you're wrong. I am casting myself at your feet. I do cast myself at your feet."

Joan's eyes were wide with astonishment. "You mean you want to marry me?"

"I mean I want to be your lover."

She gasped. "And Norry?"

"What Norry doesn't know isn't going to hurt him. You won't be the first woman to make love to another man during her engagement."

Joan rose and walked to the window so as to be turned away from him. "And how long would you propose that this bizarre arrangement should last?"

"As long as we both want it to. I doubt very much that you will want to continue it after you marry."

She stamped her foot. "Have you no heart at all?"

"Enough. We would be taking a gamble with our emotions, I admit. But I think we can handle it. I know I want to try."

She turned now and stared hard at him. Was it gratitude that he made out in that penetrating, dark look? "Very much?"

"Oh, yes."

"But not enough to marry me?"

"It wouldn't be right. The way for you to live is to be what you are. To accept yourself. Then your worldliness will be big and handsome. Not sordid and small."

"And Norry? Would it be fair to him?"

"Oh, honey, you'll make Norry a tremendous wife!"

She walked over to him slowly and then suddenly put her hands on his shoulders. "Will you teach me how?" She was utterly serious. "I know I look experienced, but I'm not. Not a bit!"

"You don't look as experienced as you think," he said with a chuckle. "But we can have the first lesson right now."

"Oh, darling, don't joke about it!"

"It's the only way, Joan. Believe me."

She hugged him desperately and put her head against his chest. "I don't know what I think. I guess I'd better not think at all. I guess I'd better just leave it to you."

••

During the first month of Tony's affair with Joan he met Lee Bogardus. As he saw Joan only on the nights that he visited the apartment of the Lanes, who were still in Florida, he seemed perfectly unattached in the eyes of his acquaintance. And in truth he was. There was little sentiment in his feeling for Joan. On her side there might have been more, but she was a woman of unusual power, and she stuck to her implied bargain. Besides, the plan was working. The confidence that she drew from sex made her easier and more relaxed with Norris, who was already thoroughly ashamed of his suspicion of her mercenary motives. He had even gone so far as to propose, and Joan now had her revenge by keeping *him* dangling.

Tony had been immediately drawn to Lee. Her impassioned account of the rejected short story in the little garden behind their host's brownstone had intrigued him. She had seemed hardly aware of him as a man as she told it, but as soon as his sympathy came through to her, she forgot all about her problems as a writer. Afterward, when he took her out, he was amused by the conflict between her rather quaint, old-fashioned reserve and her obvious need for a much warmer relationship. It was as if she might have been taught by her mother that "nice" girls had to prove hard to get and yet was speculating that if she didn't move a bit faster, she might lose this new beau altogether. And this was something that she very clearly did not want to let happen.

One night he insisted on coming up to the apartment, rather than waiting for her in the lobby, so that he might meet her parents. Tony loved to meet parents. Mr. and Mrs. Bogardus, a wonderfully handsome couple, he very gray and tall and distinguished, she, brilliant if falsely blonde, treated him with a formal but intense politeness. He felt immediately that he was being considered as a serious suitor and that he had already passed the first round.

"Where do your parents live, Mr. Lowder?" Lee's mother asked, after her father had shown himself perfectly satisfied with Tony's law credentials.

"They live on the West Side, Mummie," Lee interrupted rudely. "You may as well know right away that they don't have a fashionable address."

"Lee, dear child," Mrs. Bogardus breathed, in the manner of a parent quite accustomed to such ferocities, "there's nothing wrong with the West Side. I lived there myself as a child."

"Yes, but below Fifty-ninth Street. That was quite all right. I know your little rules. But Tony's family are on Central Park West."

"You don't have to defend my family's address, Lee," Tony interposed with a laugh. "We've never had any claim to being fashionable. Quite the reverse. On Daddy's side we were Jewish at the wrong time, and on Mother's Catholic. We're always out of step."

"You mean you're not Catholic now?" Mrs. Bogardus asked, with what her daughter undoubtedly construed as relief.

"No, we're nothing. We're Episcopalians."

Mr. and Mrs. Bogardus exhanged undecipherable glances. He, smiling, now resumed the questioning. "Didn't your mother's family object to such apostasy?"

"Not really. To the Irish religion is essentially politics. So long as we remain loyal to the tribe . . ." Tony shrugged. "Well, nobody much cared."

Lee was obviously a bit shocked, but Tony had the feeling that her parents were not. There was a bleak little communion between him and the Bogarduses. It was only Lee who cared for things past.

She was certainly ready for marriage. Ready and more than ready. It must have been bad enough for her to know this herself, without having it made quite so obvious that her parents knew it too. Tony could sense in the Bogarduses' welcome of him their willingness to waive all requirements of residence and genealogy in the interest of getting off their hands into those of any decently respectable male a daughter who was probably moody and violent behind the scenes. Let us *do* something, their worried eyes seemed to plead, before she goes off with the elevator boy!

Of course, they were unjust to her. He quite saw that. They knew nothing about girls. Far from being about to go off with the elevator boy, poor Lee did not dare even show him the inclination that she obviously did feel. When he took her home after an evening she would almost scramble out of the taxi in her effort not to look as if she were waiting for a good night kiss. He let her go, but sometimes, later in the same night, when he made love to Joan, he would think of Lee.

Lee seemed to suspect something. He could see that she was troubled by his slowness in making advances. Was he involved with another girl? Was he queer?

"You listen so well," she told him in a bar after a Saturday afternoon concert. "You listen to music the way you listen to people. You really hear."

"Is that rare?"

"I think it is. It makes me feel I can ask you something without your taking it wrong. Without your thinking . . ." She paused, much embarrassed.

"Thinking what?"

"Well, that I'm throwing myself at you," she said almost defiantly. "I couldn't bear that."

"I promise not to think it, then. What did you want to ask me?"

There was another rather breathless pause. "I wanted to ask you if you think it's funny that a girl my age—twenty-three—has never, well never . . ."

"Had an affair? Funny? You mean, do I think it's unusual? No."

Lee was taken aback by his casualness. "How did you know I was going to ask that?"

"Wasn't it obvious?"

"That I was so . . . pure?"

"No, no. That it was on your mind."

"Well, I've heard that a man has to be experienced that way before he's married or else he'll be a terrible fumbler. Mightn't it be true of a woman, too?"

Tony laughed. "Those things aren't difficult to learn. You'll find it will come very easily."

Lee jumped up at this and hurried to the ladies' room. When she came back, it was evident that she had been weeping.

"You *do* think I've thrown myself at you. I've never been so humiliated in my life. Please take me home."

"May I tell you something first?"

"No. Please. I'll just start crying again."

"Let me say one thing."

"Tony, I want to go!"

"All right." He signaled to the waiter. "But you'll have to have dinner with me tomorrow night. I don't for a minute think that you're throwing yourself at me. It's still possible, however, that I may want to throw myself at you. And I think you should give me the chance."

••

Later that night, as Joan and Tony were lying, smoking cigarettes, on her mother's bed, which they used because it was larger than her own, and the room more comfortable than hers, he asked her about Norry.

"When are you going to give him his answer?"

"Soon, I suppose. I've wanted to prolong our 'idyll.' Oh, Tony, do you think we mustn't meet afterward?"

"Not for a time, anyway. You have to give him a chance. He'll probably be a marvelous lover."

"But I'll be thinking of you when he makes love to me."

"No, you won't. Not after a time."

"And you'll be after some other girl."

"Naturally."

"Someone you'll want to marry?"

"I hope so."

"Damn you, Tony!"

"Now don't get excited."

"You don't know anything about women!"

"We agreed this was an experiment. It wasn't guaranteed to work."

"But you were a bastard to try such an experiment."

"Oh, that's for sure."

"And that's what helps me. Would I really want to be married to such a bastard?"

"And would I want to be married to a girl who two-times her boy friend?"

"Ah, there you are!" Joan laughed a bit wildly. "I guess you are a bit of a genius, lover. You've made me accept something no woman would accept. No decent woman, that is."

Just then the telephone rang sharply in Tony's ear. Joan reached across him to pick it up, and he listened to her conversation with Norris, the cord stretched tight against his jugular vein. Norris, who had obviously been drinking, sounded loud and angry.

"What are you doing?"

"What do you mean, what am I doing? I've gone to bed, that's what I'm doing. What the hell are *you* doing, calling at this hour?"

"It's only eleven."

"Oh, is that all? Well, anyway, I was asleep, and it's horrid to be wakened up when you've just gone to sleep. Particularly by rude drunks."

"I'm sorry, Joanie darling." Norris's voice dropped

to a whine. "I'm not drunk. I had a few at the club because somebody told me you were going out with Tony again."

"I *am* going out with Tony again. Have I ever made a secret of it?"

"Ah, honey, don't you know what that does to me? It kills me, that's all."

"There's no reason it should kill you. Tony's a very dear friend of mine. Any man I marry is going to have to get used to Tony. If you think, Norris Conway, that I'm the kind of woman you can lock up in a harem guarded by some eunuch, you have another think coming."

Norris's voice became very excited at this. "Oh, honey, does that mean you *might* marry me? You could have everything the way you want it. Honest! I don't mind your having friends—that is, if they are friends."

"If you're going to insult me now . . ."

"Please, honey, no! Tell me I have just a chance, and I'll hang right up."

"You have just a chance."

"Oh, darling! Let me come up. Let me come up just for one minute and give you just one kiss, that's all, and I swear on a million bibles I'll go straight home, the happiest man in the world!"

"I tell you, I'm in bed, Norris!" Joan sounded scandalized.

"Get up and put your wrapper on. You won't have to do more than open the door. I'll take one kiss and go."

"My parents are away!"

"I tell you what then. I'll make the elevator man wait. How's that?"

Joan hesitated. "Where are you?"

"At the drugstore on the corner."

"All right, but remember. One kiss. And the elevator man waits."

Tony replaced the receiver that she silently handed to him. She switched on the light, hurried to the bureau and sat down to comb her hair in short, sharp strokes. Then she put on a nightgown and a silk wrapper, firmly tying the cord.

"What do I do?" he demanded. "Get under the bed?"

"You stay right where you are," she snapped. "The door will be closed."

"Suppose he comes in to look?"

"Then he's not a man I care to marry." She cast an almost contemptuous look at him. "Are you afraid?"

Tony laughed. "Not unless he has a gun!"

The front door buzzer sounded, and Joan went out, switching the light off as she did so. Tony jumped out of bed and stood by the bedroom door which she had closed. On the other side was the living room, which opened directly into the hall foyer.

"You see, the elevator man is waiting." Norris's voice came to him. "I promise to be a good boy. One kiss, and I'm gone." Tony heard the kiss.

"All right, Norry, that's enough."

"And you *may* marry me?"

"Yes, I think I really may."

"You mean you *will* marry me?"

"I'll tell you tomorrow."

"Oh, Joan! You darling!"

"Good night, Norry." Her tone was cool, sure, almost domestic.

There was the sound of another kiss, and then of

a closing door. Joan opened the bedroom door and stood there, silhouetted against the living room light. He came up, naked, to embrace her.

"You're a remarkable woman!"

She pushed him away. "And I suppose you think you're a remarkable man." Her voice was dry and flat. "Maybe you are. But not a man to marry. Oh, I see that now! Clear out of here, will you? And go down the stairs and out the back way."

"You think he may be waiting?"

"No. He's a gentleman. Something I'm afraid you know very little about. I don't want the elevator man to see you. I could never face him!"

••

The next night, at seven o'clock, Tony waited for Lee downstairs in the lobby. When he saw her coming from the elevator down the long corridor he moved forward to meet her. She stopped, and he kissed her. As he did so, he had the faint sensation of Inez Feldman's sticky, gum-droppy kiss in the conservatory of her father's mansion of Riverside Drive when he had paid up for his immunity in the theft of the dolls' house divan. But when he drew his head back and saw Lee's eyes, scared, questioning, as if dreading some brutal hurt, he kissed her again, more searchingly, and there were no gum drops. Then he kissed her a third time, right in front of the old doorman, who had come in from the street and whom she had known from childhood. That Lee, transparently the kind of girl who should object to such a witness, did not object, went far toward convincing Tony how utterly he was at last committed.

5

Lee's parents went to bed very early, and Pieter Bogardus was already asleep when Tony called. As soon as he began to make out the extraordinary nature of his son-in-law's communication and heard the terms "Regional Director" and "S.E.C." he shut him right up and told him to come downtown the next day for lunch. Then he went back to sleep. Pieter was a man who could do this.

He had a private metaphor to describe life—his own life, anyway (it might or might not describe the life of others)—which he had never disclosed to anyone, not even to Lee's mother. To him it was a dusty, drafty tunnel with nothing at the end but the source of all the dust and drafts. Yet it was a happy paradox that this seemingly bleak philosophy never depressed him. Pieter had always been willing to decorate his tunnel with rugs and draperies, with chandeliers and tapestries, to convert its turnings into Turkish corners, its dust into gold dust. The secret, he had discovered early, was to cover over every square inch of floor or wall and to keep them covered. The process, to be sure, was endless, for every least relaxation was followed by a peeling, a stripping, a blast of dirty wind, and even such necessary refreshment as a night's sleep was bound to be paid for by anxious periods of needed and busy repair. But to the careful and industrious there could come moments of reward, moments of near ecstasy, moments indeed when life was almost bare of apprehension.

Adapting his metaphor to his own body, Pieter found that shaving, combing, brushing, bathing, dressing were essential and agreeable parts of the ritual. Not only did they undo the ravages of night; they acted as shields against the garish day. Then Pieter Bogardus, with smooth gray hair about a gleaming scalp and a serene, handsome, classical face, a face that might be gazing down from a Gilbert Stuart or a Rembrandt Peale, could take his place at the breakfast table overlooking the busy East River, pour his coffee from a George II urn and turn away from the rugged headlines to the relative order of the obituary page.

He had long given up making any effort to change the popular image of himself as it existed among his friends and law associates. They thought of him as a descendant of Pieter Stuyvesant who took a great, perhaps an inordinate, pride in the fact, as a person of aristocratic tastes who cared very much for forms and traditions, as a martinet with a kindly heart and a redeeming twinkle in the eye. Why carp at such an image? Was it not finer, after all, than the fact, finer than the image of a man who was indifferent to all forms, all traditions, a man who cared for no one on earth but his wife, a man who dressed and lived carefully because only through personal order and neatness could he hope to arrange his tunnel so it would pass inspection? Inspection by whom? Ah, who knew? Maybe by the monster that crouched at the end of the tunnel and exhaled all the drafts and dust.

Pieter could tell you what he had paid for butter in any year and how many days their general maid had taken off the winter before. Pieter totaled up his sales taxes for the correct deduction and kept a little black book in his vest pocket to note such charitable contributions as might lurk in the entrance fees to entertainments or exhibitions. Pieter filed all reports and returns to every insurance company or governmental agency at least ten days in advance. To run a home properly in the "age of forms," as he called it, was a task that excluded most other activities. Pieter and Selena rarely went out in the evening and never went away for a weekend. Every summer they went to Narragansett in the same week in July and returned in the same week in August. On Thanksgiving and Christmas they attended divine service. They were punctilious about funerals.

People were always under the illusion that Pieter would approve of them if they were neat and disapprove of them if they were messy. They could never understand that he didn't give a damn *how* they looked. He had quite enough to do getting through his own life without bothering how they got through theirs. And who knew? Perhaps they were judged by other criteria. Perhaps they were exempt. Perhaps they did not have to live in tunnels.

Selena did not leave her room until eleven, and

Pieter did not have to speak at breakfast except to bid the maid a courteous good-morning. After his coffee and boiled egg he did household accounts for half an hour and then walked to the subway, where he took the last car, obliterating the actual dark, dusty tunnel by reading advance sheets of tax cases. Walking down the long corridor to his office he greeted those whom he passed cheerily enough, but nobody ever stopped to ask a question or tell a story or comment on the weather. It was too well known that Mr. Bogardus wanted to go straight to his room where he could close the door and not emerge until he went to the toilet at nine-forty-five. If one had anything to say to him, one did so between eleven-thirty and his departure for his lunch club at twelve-fifteen. If the Commissioner of Internal Revenue himself had called at twelve-fourteen, he would have been told that Mr. Bogardus would take no calls until two.

Oh, people thought he was funny. Of course, he knew that. Where would people have been in the dead world of downtown if they had not had eccentrics like him to laugh at, to feel superior to? He could imagine, with total indifference, what they must say to themselves: "Look at him, a descendant of Pieter Stuyvesant, a successful tax lawyer, a social registerite, and rather a dear old boy, but for all his advantages what is he really but a poor slave obsessed with dates and forms and minor obligations, hipped on having a spotless blotter for his desk and a regularly emptied colon? And look at me—a stenographer, an office boy, a clerk, a cleaning woman—do *I* clutter my life up with such senseless details?" Don't you? Pieter smiled grimly as he put the question to his imagined mockers. Such people, like as not, had nothing in their lives to cling to but liquor and television and a bit of sex, equating the pleasure of any slut in orgasm with the ecstasy of a saint. What could such creatures know of ecstasy?

"Yes, darling, how are you?" he asked into the speaker when Selena called. She called every morning at eleven, after she finished her face. Selena at sixty, had the gold hair and alabaster complexion of a woman half her age, but she had to work for it. "Of course, I remember where you put it. It's under the pin dish on your bureau. Don't forget, it's to be used for clothes. Every penny of it." Selena and he were entirely agreed about the minimum social life for the evening, but she lunched every day at her club, and she liked to look well for the girls. "And if you're tired, skip the hospital meeting this afternoon. Why don't you go to the movies?"

She left him to *his* pleasure, to the review of the *Ellison* case, and the memoranda prepared by two clerks. If the trustees of the late Anabel Ellison had had the power to invade principal for her benefit, and if the late Anabel Ellison had been vested with the power to remove and replace such trustees, had that constituted such a power in her as to place the trust in her taxable estate? Pieter's eyes blinked slowly as his mind began to run down the scent. Couldn't Anabel have kept appointing new trustees until she had found one compliant to her wishes? In fact, yes, but in law? Could a trustee be presumed to be compliant? Could he be presumed to be a bad trustee?

Pieter rose suddenly and clapped his hand to his heart. Tony! He had just remembered Tony and the hideous telephonic revelation of the night before. Then, quite deliberately, he made himself breathe slowly and regularly, as by an old disciplinary process he turned his mind firmly from the thought. There was never any point dwelling on disaster before one had to. He was breaking one rule already that day by lunching with Tony. Enough was enough. God!

He sat down again to resume his review of the *Ellison* case. Thirty-five years before, when his father's estate, already depleted by the 1929 crash, had been finally obliterated by the federal estate tax, Pieter had abandoned stock brokerage to study law. Upon graduation he had declared his private war against the Treasury which he had faithfully fought ever since. Never, by articles in law reviews or by speeches at tax forums, had he given the least intelligence to the enemy. Never had he served on committees of bar associations advising the government on tax legislation. All his cases had been against the nation, and to have helped the latter in the smallest way to draft better laws or to find better taxing officers would have been, by his lights, simple treason.

"Mr. Lowder called," his secretary telephoned from the next room. "He'll be here at noon."

"I'll see him at twelve-ten," he snapped. "We'll walk together to the Down Town Association."

Damn Tony Lowder. The typescript of the memorandum wriggled before him, and he saw his son-in-law behind bars. Good. *Good?* No, no! He panted as he again forced his mind, like a reluctant wheelchair, to turn about and face down the boardwalk to the Ellison problem. Ah, yes. But even if a trustee would not be deemed to be a compliant trustee, might not the power to appoint any trustee be deemed the power in Anabel to appoint herself? And if Anabel were the trustee, acting with a nonadverse party, possessed of this power . . .

But hush. He flicked over the pages of the memorandum. No, the point was not made. These young men always missed the most beautiful things. Wasn't there a New York statute that prohibited a trustee from exercising a power for his own benefit? Of course there was. Oh, how beautiful it was . . .

It was time to go to the john. One pleasure could await another. He would go to the john and read the proof of his article on taxation of short-term trusts which he had reserved for just that time, and then he would have the pleasure of going to the library to look up that law and after that the delight of pointing out (oh so charmingly, so easily, so tolerantly) to the young man what he had missed. He hesitated before opening the lavatory door. Would that awful office boy who always hummed tunes be in the adjoining toilet? Really, it was intolerable, this common use of the washroom, this democracy of defecation. He would have to speak to the office manager . . . but no, all the toilets were vacant. A perfect morning.

Or it might have been.

At precisely twelve-ten, he went out to greet Tony in the reception hall. They walked together silently to the Down Town Association. At table it was Tony, the guest, who nonetheless suggested a drink.

"You go ahead," Pieter said coldly. "You know I never do before lunch."

"I thought today you might."

"Not even today."

They had a table in an alcove where they could not be overheard. Tony told his horrid tale. He had already given Pieter the bare facts on the telephone. There were not many to add. Pieter listened with a grave attention behind which his legal mind rapidly calculated the chances of Tony's being caught. Fortunately, they seemed slight.

"Well, I don't suppose you've come to me for a lecture," he said, with a little sigh, when he had heard it all. "It's a sick, tragic business, but I take it you know all that. Your conscience is your own best punishment. What can I say? Keep your nose clean in the future, and you'll be all right."

"You mean I should just do nothing?"

"What the devil *can* you do?"

"What about the bribe money?"

Pieter shrugged. "I suppose eventually you can give it to charity. One of your boys' clubs, perhaps." He suddenly thought of something almost pleasant. "Or Mrs. Bogardus's hospital."

"I wish it were as simple as that."

"What are you talking about? Of course, it's as simple as that. It's the only way it can be."

"I'm sorry, Mr. Bogardus, but you've never been in a jam like mine."

"I should hope not." Pieter did not at all like the preoccupied way with which Tony fingered the silver by his plate. He began to wonder if pressure and guilt might not have unsettled the younger man's mind. "Look, Tony," he continued in a milder tone, and Pieter could be very mild, very sympathetic, when he chose—indeed even gracious. Why did people hate that word? Because they thought it was hypocritical? He wasn't hypocritical. He *liked* Tony. "Look, my boy, I can understand that you want to make some reparation for your breach of public trust. Indeed, I should be sorry if you did not feel that way. But be practical. There is no way you can do it. It isn't like restoring stolen property. Whom could you give the money back to? The crooks who bribed you? The Securities and Exchange Commission?"

"Oh, no, I've given up all idea of restitution. You're perfectly right, of course. There's no easy way out of this. But there's still a way."

"And what is that?"

"I can go to the United States Attorney and make a full confession."

As soon as Tony had said this, Pieter realized that all along he had known it was coming. That was what the gray look in Tony's eyes and on his face had meant. Tony was no longer satisfied to live as sane men lived. He was going now to start tearing up and down his tunnel, ripping cloths and tapestries. But did he stop for a second to consider what this might do to the neighboring tunnels?

"Have you thought of Lee? Have you thought of Eric and Isabel? Have you thought of your mother and father?"

"I've thought of them, of course. I have a lifetime of that kind of thinking behind me. But the point is: I have to be a person they respect. Jesus Christ told his disciples there should be nobody between him and them: no wife or child or parent. That always used to shock me, but now I think I see what he meant. There shouldn't be anyone between a man and his conscience. If there is, it's really because he's using them as an excuse. I've used Lee as an excuse ever since we married. And I used my mother and father as excuses before that."

Pieter was scandalized. To talk about Christ in the Down Town Association was grossly improper. People who talked about Christ in that way were always very odd people indeed. Like as not half of them had committed some hideous crime. Crime? Pieter almost jumped from his seat. It came over him for the first time that his son-in-law really *was* a criminal.

"I think we had better keep your religious principles to yourself," he said coldly. "I have little understanding of such matters. What I see are half-a-dozen lives ruined to satisfy a crazy scruple and no good accomplished. Think of yourself, if you won't think of those you've brought into the world. Think of what you'll be doing to your own potential to do good. You'll never be trusted again. You'll never get another decent job. But if you keep your mouth shut and go back to work in a spirit of true repentance, you may still accomplish great things. You may even find that your experience in wrong-doing has given you a clue to helping others."

"Let me tell you a little bit about myself, Mr. Bogardus," Tony suggested. They still had not ordered, but Tony seemed totally uninterested in eating. Pieter, with another sigh, waved away the headwaiter who was approaching. "It might help you to understand me," Tony continued. "For days after I had my experience at the Conways', I lived in a kind of hell. It was something more horrible than anything I had ever imagined. All the normal limits of suffering seemed to have been lifted. The world was cold and dirty-dark, and I knew I couldn't even escape it by dying. I thought of suicide, but that just didn't seem a solution. I don't know if I consciously believed that my suffering would survive death. I doubt it. It was more that I had a funny conviction that suicide wasn't open to me. It wasn't in the cards, in the order of things, and that was that. I was going to have to go on living in this unbearably bleak world indefinitely, forever—I don't know—but anyway with no visible means of cessation. I was condemned to live in a world of Tony Lowders. For in the next few days the people I saw began to turn into *me*. That was it: I had somehow turned the world into a world of people who had done what I'd done and who didn't care. Didn't care that they'd done it or that I'd done it. Do you see it at all?"

"Not at all."

Tony shrugged. "Why should you? You've never committed a felony. You've never even committed a misdemeanor."

"Should I be ashamed of that?"

"Oh, no, believe me, sir, no. But let me go on. Or are you hungry?"

"Go on."

"Well, realizing that I had condemned myself to live in such a world, with such people, was . . . well, as I say, it was hell. There was no longer any goal worth attaining. What was the use of money or political success in such a world? What was the point of bringing up children to live in such a world? How could one love in such a world? Love anyone, even Lee? For hadn't she, too, become a part of it?"

"You were speaking . . . you were speaking of Jesus." Pieter looked about to be sure again they could not be overheard. "Did you go to church? Did you try prayer?"

"I did. I prayed. Then I sought comfort in atheism and in ideas of personal extinction. Nothing did any good. It was not until I gave up trying to escape that I escaped at all. Not until I decided that there was no hope for me of any kind, that I was doomed to go on as I was going and that that was that. And then, one night when I had been working late, I came home and found that Lee had already gone to bed and was asleep. Poor Lee, what hell she's been through, too. But I couldn't help her. Anyhow, I went into the dining room and poured myself a drink. But as I was sitting at the table, after only one swallow, I had a sudden sense of silence around me. A special silence. The kind of silence I used to love on fishing trips in the Canadian woods. The balm, the relief, was sublime. I sat there in a trance of surprise and delight. I didn't even have any more of my drink. I was too afraid of breaking the spell. For the first time in days there was no pain in my heart. And then, all of a sudden, I was filled with a sense of inexpressible well-being. Of love, you might call it."

"Did you see anything?" Pieter was curious in spite of himself.

"A presence? A ghost? No. Nor did I hear anything. I simply had the oddest feeling that all around me were layers and layers of reassurance. If was quite fantastic. Really, I *knew* that my guilt would be expiated. How, I didn't know or even much care. All I had to do was be patient and in time I would see."

"Which is what you do now?"

"Which is what I do now."

"You see that you must confess?"

"Just so."

"And why, pray, do you tell *me?*"

"Because you're Lee's father. Because you'll have to help her and the children when I go to jail."

"Thanks! Have you told her?"

"No. But I will tonight."

Pieter knew that he would have to control his pounding indignation so long as there was the smallest chance of dissuading this lunatic. "Has it occurred to you that this impulse may be self-pity? That it may be a need to dramatize yourself?"

"I don't care. All I know is that I'm going to obey it. When I tell you, Mr. Bogardus, that the distress to my family, the humiliation of public disgrace and the misery of going to jail are as *nothing* compared to the hell I was in, will you realize the force of what has happened to me?"

Pieter viewed the distracted man now with eyes of unconcealed detestation. "Of course, you attribute your impulse not to your bowels or to your psyche but to the intercession of Christ."

"Or Jupiter. Or Osiris. I don't know. I don't care. I attribute it to whatever you want to call it."

"I don't think you'd care to know what I want to call it!" Pieter allowed some of his outrage to escape in the near shout that he now addressed to the hovering headwaiter: "Could you bring us menus, please? We've been waiting long enough, I guess."

6

Lee sat with Mrs. Catlin at the long table of the board room of the Turtle Bay Settlement House. One end of the table, unoccupied except by them, was covered with neatly stacked copies of lists and prospectuses. Mrs. Catlin's bright little secretary with her mane of black hair and those wide eyes under big glasses, that might have been mocking or might have been simply bored, sat at a desk, sucking a pencil tip, listening to them.

"You will see on this list that I have projected not only the anticipated gifts of the people whom you will approach, but what I estimate their 'outreach' to be: that is, what they might be expected to get from the people whom *they* approach."

Mrs. Catlin's tone was soft, warm, dream-like, suited to her faded, melancholy, aristocratic appearance. She might have been an old infanta, long living in exile. Her patience, like her research, knew no bounds. She gave to her profession of money-raising a kind of tattered dignity, like old lace on a wedding gown.

"You will notice that I have placed a number of 'old' New Yorkers on your list. They tend to be overlooked these days with all the emphasis on new money. But plenty of them are still very well off. Their trouble is that they think traditionally in terms of small gifts. They are apt not to take in what the tax deduction really means to them."

"I see you have Daddy on the list. What on earth gave you that idea? He never gives anything except to Mummie's hospital. It's a matter of principle."

"My dear, there's always a first time for everybody. If I'd given up with the first person I'd been told was hopeless, I'd have gone out of business years ago. Your father is very proud of you and Tony . . ."

Lee closed her eyes and smiled as she tried to imagine what her future "outreach" would be, once Tony had confessed. "Mrs. Anthony Lowder? Lowder? Didn't he go to jail or something? Wasn't it that bribery case?" Oh, Tony, beloved Tony, how I love you! How I bless you for telling me what you told me last night. It was absurd—it was obscene—to be so happy with ruin staring one in the eyes. But what did it all prove but that love, poor, battered, knocked-about love, love, the false premise of suburban America, the only point of pointless lives, the indispensable guest at the cocktail party, the bridge party, the cookout—indispensable but never appearing, the ghost of Banquo that never came, that this very love, in short, was true? She hardly heard Mrs. Catlin's voice.

"Are you all right, dear?"

"Oh, I'm fine. I was just thinking of my outreach." She glanced again at her list, and her eye fell on the Cs. "You want *me* to approach Joan Conway?"

It would have been more natural, she reflected, if Mrs. Catlin had exchanged glances with Miss Paul. She felt the falsity of their not doing so.

"You think Tony would be better? Mrs. Conway is supposed to prefer the gentlemen."

Really, Belle Catlin was too perfect. It was just the right answer. She knew everything about Joan and Tony, of course. Everything and nothing. For she had no inkling of the wonderful scene between Lee and Tony of the night before. And even when she should learn of it, or of its consequences, she would still know nothing. For she would never understand that out of the gray walls and bars of public misery would spring a Kundry's garden of hope and rebirth. It was to Lee as if she and Tony had died and survived their own deaths. Now she inhabited the old body of Lee Lowder, and the old Lee Lowder gave the appearance of continuing to communicate with the world, but she, the real she, was existing on a different level of reality, and she and Tony would make forays out of the impregnable citadel of their new happiness to smile sadly at this darkened old world. Had Belle Catlin ever known love? The faded gleam in her melancholy eyes suggested that she had. But it must have been long ago.

"Tony won't talk to her about money," Lee said. "She's sick, you know."

"I hear she's dying," Mrs. Catlin said softly.

"We all are," Lee retorted. "At least, we all were."

"Maybe it's better to wait for the will. But I

doubt if there's anything in it. Mrs. Conway has never really cared for settlement houses. She only does what she does because of Tony. Museums are more her line. I think you'd better talk to her, Lee. Unless, of course, you can persuade Tony to change his mind."

Lee looked up in surprise. It suddenly seemed as if Belle Catlin were far away, as if the table surface between them had multiplied by several leaves. "He's not having an affair with her, you know," she heard herself say.

"Who?"

"My husband. With Joan. That's all over now."

This time Mrs. Catlin did look at Miss Paul. "Leave us a minute, will you, Rhoda?"

Miss Paul left the room without a word.

"What's wrong, dear?" Mrs. Catlin asked, in the same soft tone.

"Nothing. It's as I say, that's all. It wasn't because of the affair that he wouldn't approach her. It was because he wanted her to have one relationship that wasn't connected with her money. I wonder if you can understand that, Belle?"

"Of course, I can understand it."

"You say that, and you believe it. You're perfectly sincere. You're always sincere. But your philosophy has a flaw in it." Lee felt detached, almost numb, as she proceeded. "You believe it's all right to cultivate people for their money if the purpose is charity. But actually it's more contaminating than if the purpose is personal. Because your illusion of safety puts you at the mercy of the microbe. The microbe of evil. You and I and Tony are mendicants, Belle, pure and simple. We fawn. We smile. We dine out in rich houses like Joan Conway's. If we did for ourselves what we do for charity, the whole world would revile us."

Mrs. Catlin did not smile or frown. She simply nodded. "Go ahead, dear. Get it off your chest. We all feel that way from time to time. And what's more, there's a good deal of truth in it."

"Forgive me, Belle. I've made a bloody ass of myself."

"Something's happened to you, Lee. I won't ask you because I know you won't tell me. But let me say this. I like you. I respect you. And I'm sorry."

"Oh, Belle." In contrition she rose and went over to kiss her. "Why do you always have to be so right even when you're so wrong?"

"Anyway, we'll drop the subject of your list. For now, anyway. Why don't you go over this membership brochure while I check the mailing? I'd love to get it out this afternoon."

Lee knew that the brochure would be perfect, but she seized it, as if to cover her nakedness. She took it away to an armchair in the corner to escape Belle's immediate scrutiny and, with a quick sigh of relief, let her mind fill up again with the strange bliss of the night before. Tony's face, large and lined, grave as she had never seen it, yet with an odd kind of new confidence, almost of cockiness, seemed to cover over the whole proscenium of her imagination, like a giant poster at a political rally. He had talked, and at first she had only half listened, about a complicated office matter. When at last she had begun to understand, she had listened passionately. And then it had all come clear: his abstraction, his seeming indifference, his bottomless misery, his amazing decision.

"Your father was naturally first concerned about

you and the children," he had told her. "Of course, it's going to be ghastly for all of you. Isabel may get through by dramatizing it. Eric will have a much harder time. I can hardly bear to think of Eric. But I'm banking on his intellect. I'm hoping that he'll be able to rationalize it."

"And me? How do I face it?"

"By loving me."

"Oh, Tony," she had whispered.

"I've thought and thought about it. At first I wondered if I shouldn't give you a chance to change your and the children's name, to leave me and go to another part of the country. Your father suggested that."

"Daddy did?"

"Oh, yes, he hates me now, poor man. I can't blame him. If he could wish me dead, I'm sure he would."

"No, Tony!"

"Yes, darling. See it his way. He thought his daughter was off his hands and permanently looked after. He was even beginning to see a prospect of something like success in his unlikely son-in-law's future career. At *long* last. So he and your mother could look forward in peace to the uninterrupted bliss of totting up Gristede bills and trying to catch the bank in error in its monthly statements. And then what happens? For a crazy scruple the idiot Lowder blows the works and throws his family, disgraced, back on the old man's payroll."

And then, incredibly, they had both laughed. The hope that he had kindled so many years before at the dull little brownstone garden cocktail party of their first meeting, the hope that a Bogardus world of downtown grays and military browns might blur and dissolve into a turbulent riot of shrieking colors, of imperial abstracts, the hope that romance had a validity outside of good nineteenth-century fiction and bad twentieth-century movies, the hope that everything within her that she had ever tried to repress or of which she might have felt ashamed could erupt instead into orgasm, physical, mental, spiritual, the hope in every daughter that she was real and her parents bogus, was alive again.

"Oh, darling," she gasped, "I see it all. If you only *knew* how I see it all. There's nothing, absolutely nothing, that you and I can't work out if we work it out together. Of course, it's going to be terrible for Isabel and Eric." She closed her eyes in a spasm of horror as she thought indeed how terrible it would be for Eric. Yet it passed, the dreadful moment. It actually passed. She took a breath and went on. "But in the long run they'll realize what an incredibly brave thing you've done, and they'll admire you for it. Oh, they will, Tony. Who else would give up what you'll be giving up? Freely? Without the least pressure? Without any danger of discovery? Oh, the time will come when they'll boast about you. For what is there really to be ashamed of? You performed an experiment in human psychology. You wanted to create yourself, and you *did*. You wanted to become a bribed man, and that is just what you did become. And having become one, you faced the consequences. I've always loved you, but I've never admired you more."

But when they had gone to bed that night, making love had seemed more real than what he had told her.

"What do you think of it?" Belle Catlin asked.

"What do I think of *what?*"

"The brochure, darling. The brochure. Not whatever it was you were dreaming about. I wouldn't think of intruding *there.*"

"The brochure is perfect."

"Nonsense. You haven't read a word of it."

"That doesn't mean it's not perfect."

"Why don't you go home, Lee? You're obviously not going to get any work done today."

"I'm going to read the brochure!" Lee cried passionately, and she turned abruptly away from Belle.

She had slept heavily the night before, dreamlessly, a kind of love death. She must have dreaded her awakening, for when she had opened her eyes in the harsh light she had given a little cry of alarm.

"Darling, I'm right here." Tony was standing by the bed with a shaving brush in his hand.

"Oh, Tony, hold me!" she cried in panic. "Hold me, and tell me it's all right. That it's going to *be* all right."

He sat down on the edge of the bed and held her close.

"Thank you," she breathed. "When are you going to do it? Confess, I mean?"

"I have to speak to Max first."

"Max? Why Max?" She was wide awake now and throbbing with immediate jealousy. "What has Max to do with it?"

Tony looked at her in surprise. "Well, I guess *he* thinks he has something to do with it. I've got to work it out so as not to involve him. Of course, I won't give his name, but once the thing's out, the

U. S. Attorney's office can be expected to run him down. I'll try to make a deal for him, but he may find it advisable to arrange a business trip to Brazil. Until it all blows over."

"A deal for Max! What about a deal for you?"

"Well, I don't say that's impossible. It has been known for first offenders who turn themselves in to get suspended sentences. I'm not going to beg them to send me to jail. But with Max it's different. There's no reason that Max should suffer for my conscience when he's lucky enough to have none of his own."

"Well, I think there is." Lee could not abide the intrusion of Max into their strange new purgatory, just halfway between heaven and hell. "Max was responsible for the whole wretched business. He tempted you. He wheedled you into it. No, worse, he made you feel so sorry for him that you went into it to save him! Oh, how I loathe Max!" The golden canvas of Tony's heroism seemed to be crumpling at the corners, as if it were on fire. She put a hand to her mouth to keep from screaming. If she had to go through this hideous trial on Max's moral level, it would be more than a soul could bear. "All right, go to Max," she argued with controlled vehemence. "Tell him you've decided to go to the U. S. Attorney's office. Give him the chance to go with you. That's fair enough, isn't it? And if he won't, to hell with him!"

"Lee." Tony put his hands on her bare shoulders and held her firmly. "Let me do this my way, will you? I promise you, it will be the honorable way. Trust me."

She shuddered and then clung to him for a desperate embrace. She was still thinking of that embrace, trying to get back into it, to cover herself over with it as if it were some great dark hood, while she sat with Belle's brochure in her lap. She jumped up, startled, when Belle lightly touched her shoulder.

"Please go home, Lee. Your nerves are so tight. It makes my jumpy just to watch you."

Lee threw her arms about her and sobbed. "Oh, Belle, would you still speak to me if I went to jail?"

Belle was never at a loss. She patted Lee gently on the back and let her continue to hug her. "I think I would."

"No matter what I'd done?"

"Oh, I wouldn't dream of knowing."

"But if you did?"

"I'd be sure you'd had a very compelling reason."

Lee closed her eyes as she visualized Eric's pained, bewildered face. Was anything worth that? Anything that had to be shared with Max Leonard? And would they ever be through with it, even after the jail was over? What about those criminals who had bribed Tony? Wouldn't they follow him? Wouldn't they try to get him? Or the children? Hadn't she read horrors?

"Oh, Belle, you must think I'm mad! Perhaps I am, a bit. No, I'm not going to jail. Nobody is. I was just thinking of the part of your brochure that deals with the program for exconvicts. It's very well put. Very moving. I was thinking what a hard time they must have and how important it is for us to help them."

Belle released herself from Lee's embrace and surveyed her with a critical little smile. "My God, you *did* read the brochure."

"Of course, I did."

"Lee, you're remarkable."

"I read it, and I was swept away. It should swamp us with new memberships."

She felt worthy of Tony again as she turned to the mailing list. It was going to be difficult to breathe in this new altitude, but it was obviously only by learning that she would survive.

7

The Max Leonards' house in Vernon Manor, unlike its neighbors, was old—fifty years old—and had been, when they had bought it, of dark, weather-beaten shingle, designed in a vaguely Queen Anne style, attractive enough when densely surrounded by lilacs and marigolds and a small, shimmering lawn. Now, however, that it had been converted by Elaine to the standards of opulent suburbia—painted light gray with picture windows, filled with bird prints and imitation French provincial furniture—now that it was bare and clean and bordered by a rock garden, it was as dull as Elaine herself.

Max was perfectly able to assess his own responsibility for the changes in her. He was even able to derive a dry satisfaction in his own perspicacity. After all, he and she had been caught in the same net. Elaine had never guessed, when she had married the prettiest senior at Williams, the boy with the sunniest disposition, that she had mated with a driven creature, a compulsively industrious aspirant to riches and power. It might have been better, but only a little better, had he achieved them. As it was, Elaine, neglected, had turned for a time to adultery, but not finding it a much favored vice in Vernon Manor, where husbands were jealously guarded, she had graduated to the bridge lunch at the country club, to long hours of gin and gossip with the girls. Now a failing fight with her figure had given her another occupation. The two Leonard daughters were away at boarding school. It was supposed to be a liberal one, but there were still letters from the headmistress.

Elaine never joined Max for breakfast unless she had something to dispute with him. He hated the contrast that her billowing nightgown and undone hair offered to his own matutinal neatness. Never did she less seem the American blonde beauty of their early years, an image that she could still suggest when she was dressed and made up for a party.

"Why do you suppose Tony told Governor Horton to withdraw his name from the Treasury job?"

Max glanced up from his paper. "Where did you hear that? From the girls at the club?"

"No, dear. They've never heard of Tony Lowder. He's not nearly as famous as you like to think."

"Where did you hear it, then?"

"From you. Last night. You never remember anything you tell me after the second nightcap."

Max reflected uncomfortably that this was true. It was curious that she, who drank so much more than he did, should have such total recall. It must have been because she was checking up on him.

Now that her looks were going, and he had kept his, she was afraid of losing him.

"I don't know why Tony did it," he admitted. "But I'll sure as hell find out. I'm meeting him in town today."

"May I make a suggestion?"

"Isn't that what you came down for?"

"Then I suggest your sacred Tony is self-destructive."

Max prepared himself for the latest bit of country club Freud. "Aren't we all?"

"To a lesser extent. You can tell about Tony by the way he plays bridge. He's a beautiful player, granted. But watch him through an evening when he has a winning streak. He gets progressively reckless. In the end, he's apt to be badly set on a grand slam, doubled and vulnerable."

"He likes to give the opponents a break. He's always that way in games."

"He might think of his partner."

"But that's usually Lee. She understands."

"And it's just a game. I know." Elaine seemed very sure of herself. "But I suggest that all life is a game to Tony. A game he insists on losing. And you're in for a sad disillusionment if you think Lee's his only partner. The real partner is you, sonny boy!"

Max looked at her suspiciously. Elaine could be a very insinuating woman. "What has given you this idea?"

"Watching you and Tony. Over the years. Whenever there's a noticeable disproportion between the affections of two supposedly best friends, watch out! There's trouble in store."

"You don't think Tony likes me?"

"Oh, he likes you well enough. That's not the point. The point is that what he feels about you bears no visible relation to what you feel about him. Tony's emotional life is bound up entirely with women. He has a bare tolerance for his own sex. I think I should know something about that."

"Do you imply that you've had an affair with him?"

"I imply that I could have. If I hadn't been such a faithful wife."

Max snorted. "Perhaps you misunderstood him."

"A woman doesn't misunderstand that kind of thing."

"*You* might."

Elaine flushed. "Maybe we'd understand each other better if we could talk frankly about your attitude toward Tony. Do you think we might do it impersonally? After all, we're not children."

Max shrugged without answering.

"I know he's the light of your life," Elaine continued tartly. "I've always known that. Oh, I don't say it's entirely a homosexual thing, though that's obviously part of it. People make too much of that these days. The real point is that Tony has to have all the success you haven't had. Tony has to lead *your* life. If you could ever exorcise Tony from your heart, you might discover a lot of things about yourself. You might . . ."

"I might even discover," Max interrupted angrily, "that I'm married to a woman who likes to turn a sharp knife in my guts under the cloak of a clinical discussion. Good-bye, Elaine. I'm going to my train."

••

In the Central Park Zoo, before the empty polar bear cage, Max smoked a cigarette impatiently, as if it were a task to be got through with. Tony had finished talking, for the moment anyway. He was gazing down at the seven faded wreaths piled under the sign. The bear had been shot a month before because it had seized and mauled the arm of a crazy man who had thrust a stick through the bars to annoy it. There had been no other way to make the poor beast let go of its tormentor.

"You picked a good place to meet," Max said bitterly. "You're even crazier than the guy who stuck his hand in there."

"And you feel sorry for the bear."

"Hell, I *am* the bear. I'll get shot, anyway, for your lunacy. And do you know something? I contradicted Elaine this morning when she said you liked to lose games. Well, she was right—for once in her life. You'd play Russian roulette with a cartridge in every slot."

"Except you won't be shot. You can get out of town."

"And lose my law practice? And be disbarred? Thanks, pal!"

"Don't cry before you're hurt, Max. I told you there was a good chance I could work a deal."

"A good chance! Do you realize the chance you're taking with my life? Even if you did make a deal for me, how will that square me with Lassatta? Do you think he'll ever believe I'm not a party to this crazy confession?"

"You worry too much about Lassatta. Those boys are going to have it so in for me, they won't even remember your name."

"You hope!" Max stamped his foot on the pavement in frustration. "And even if everything works out the way you say, where does that leave me? *You* were the biggest part of my plans."

"It's tough, Max. I know."

"You think it's all right to do this to me because you take the rap. But it's not, because you're getting some kind of a looney jag out of the whole thing. What's there in it for me but despair? How can you treat a friend like that?"

Tony became very grave at this. Suddenly he gripped Max's shoulder. "Why don't you come with me, Max, and confess the whole thing?"

"You *are* crazy."

"I have a kind of hunch that deep down you want to. A hunch that tells me you're sick of the whole rat race. Is it so, Max?" But Max angrily shook off his hand. "You talk about friendship," Tony continued. "Why don't you see my side? We got into this thing as friends. It was your idea to go in, and I followed you. Now it's my idea to get out. Why don't you follow me?"

"Because you're changing the terms of the friendship."

"For the better."

Max turned away abruptly and walked to the center of the zoo, stopping before the seal tank. The seals were all asleep. Tony did not follow him, probably wishing to give him the opportunity to think it out. But Max did not need to think it out. He had no intention of doing the mad thing that Tony suggested. Something had come over him that threatened to be even stronger than his fear of Lassatta. It was a hot stifled feeling in his chest and deep in his throat that made him actually cough. He was not sure what it was, but he wondered if it might not be hate.

Hate? For Tony? Was it conceivable? Of course it was conceivable! Love and hate had too much in common not to be interchangeable. But what was left of his life, then? Might he not just as well go for a ride with one of Lassatta's thugs and get it over with?

The surface of the dark water broke, and a seal's head appeared. One of them had been under, after all. Max found himself thinking of Dr. Redding, his old headmaster at St. John's, and how earnestly he had prayed in chapel. And then he thought of his mother, his darling pretty mother, Susie, who used to visit him once a term, coming up by bus and going back to New York the same day because she couldn't afford the Parents' House. How she had toiled to support him. How she had clung to the few "advantages" left after his father's death, working for a party bureau for debutantes and their ghastly mothers, until her fluttery little bird's heart had given out and he had been left alone. Could there be a more pathetic picture than that pretty boy and his pretty mother, alone against a sneering world? Laugh, will you? Screw you, brother! Max spat on the railing.

But he had been thinking of Susie at St. John's. And of Dr. Redding. For that was what he and Susie had noticed together: the way Dr. Redding prayed. He used to close his eyes tight, really tight, squeezing and crumpling his lids, and then he would shake his head heavily back and forth so that the loud rich quavery voice became more quavery, like water from a shaken garden hose. He seemed to be entering into some ecstatic private communion with God that made him forget the very service he was conducting.

"Isn't it wonderful?" Susie would whisper to Max. "You can see how real it all is to him."

Ah, yes, that was it. Susie had tried to give all the real things in life to her beloved boy by selling perfume, by modeling dresses, by arranging flowers at debuts. And seeing Dr. Redding wrestle with the God inside him had been a real thing. The idea would never have entered Susie's pretty head that there could be any relationship between Dr. Redding's God and Susie Leonard, or even between that presumably awful deity and little Max. But that was beside the point. The point was that if one wanted the real things—a good education, attractive friends and manners, a certain dash and style, and a vision of the idealism and religiosity of good teachers, or at least of headmasters—one had to pay for them. Of course, Dr. Redding was totally sincere in his convictions. He had to be. That was why his school was first class, why it cost so much.

But Tony. Was that what Tony was doing? Shaking his head, making his voice quaver, taking on the role of Dr. Redding? What damn cheek! Max strode back to him.

"How long will you give me before you go to the U. S. Attorney?"

"How long do you want?"

"I'll let you know. I'll call you."

"Max!" Tony called, for Max was already hurrying away.

"Screw you, brother." He did not turn, for he did not want to see Tony's smile.

••

Max stood in the small, bare, paneled reception room of Shea, Collins & Bogardus, specialists in tax law, and glared at the stubborn girl behind the desk.

"Mr. Bogardus never sees anyone before lunch," she insisted. "All his appointments are between two and four."

"He'll see *me*. Just tell him I've come on a matter concerning his son-in-law."

She looked doubtful. "Can't you come later?"

"Call him, will you?"

When she did this, and Mr. Bogardus's secretary came right out to take him in, he made a little face at the receptionist, and she smiled. For all his troubles he had not lost his way with women.

He did not have to ask Mr. Bogardus to close his door. The secretary did that, anyway. Tony's father-in-law, tall, strongly built, almost comically distinguished with his side ring of gray hair and gleaming high forehead, stood splendidly before him with a broad, ingratiating smile.

"And now, my dear Max, what can I do for you?" Grandly, Mr. Bogardus pointed to a chair, and both sat. "It's a long time since I've had the pleasure of seeing you."

"Tony tells me you know everything," Max blurted out. "Including his plan to confess."

The fine red lips of his host slowly retracted into an almost straight line. The large kindly eyes, blue-gray, became inscrutable. But when he spoke, his voice was gentle. "We are agreed, I hope, that it is the plan of a lunatic?"

"Entirely."

"Who must be stopped."

"Ah, but how?"

"Surely, Max, you have great influence with him?"

"No more. He was adamant. I've begged. I've argued. It's hopeless."

Mr. Bogardus looked down at his long, pink, clean fingernails as he took this in. "But Tony is very fond of you, surely. Even if he is willing to destroy himself and his famly—for some unfathomable reason of his own—must it follow that you and your family share his fate? How does he square that with his bizarre conscience?"

"He thinks he can make a deal with the U. S. Attorney that will leave me out."

"And do *you* think he can do that?"

"I don't know. He might."

"And he might not," Mr. Bogardus retorted in a harder tone that seemed to smack of something like satisfaction. "But even if he does, have you thought of where that leaves you? The U. S. Attorney, of course, is a Republican. An ambitious Republican. He will want the greatest possible publicity. Think of it from his point of view. A rising Democratic politician, whom a Republican president has been induced to consider for an assistant-secretaryship of the Treasury at the urgent persuasion of Democratic bigwigs, walks into his office, confesses to a scandalous crime and offers to collaborate in prosecuting the Mafia. What a bonanza! You can count on the U. S. Attorney to make it the case of the year and to bag as many major crooks as he can while at the same time discrediting his political opponents."

Max listened, fascinated. He saw the conclusion which Mr. Bogardus was approaching, but he could not even bring a mutter from his dry mouth.

"And where, my dear Max, I repeat, does that leave you? Even if your name is kept out of the trial, you can hardly expect that it will be unknown to a vengeful Mafia, stung to frenzy by Tony's disclosures."

"I know, I know!" Max cried with a little yelp of panic.

"So you see, my friend, you've got to stop Tony."

"How? How?"

"Can you really think of nothing?"

"Nothing. He's crazy, I tell you. There's no talking to him." Max stared at the grave blank face before him. He felt that this strange man must know a solution, but that he would not articulate it until he had drained Max dry. "I suppose I could go to Lassatta—that's the guy who started it all—and tell him what Tony's going to do," he continued desperately. "But I don't suppose we want to go that far, do we?"

"Hardly. We don't want to add murder to the list of your peccadillos." Bogardus now removed the mask and allowed his visitor to view his contempt. "No, as I see it, there's only one thing you can do to save your neck. Go to the U. S. Attorney and confess *ahead* of Tony. Demand full police protection. You'll get it. They'll do anything for you when they hear your tale. They'll even protect you permanently. They'll give you a new name, a new country, if you want. And they won't be the least interested in putting you in jail, either, because *you* weren't a public official. Mark my words, Max, you can make any deal you propose."

Max swallowed and sucked his lips for moisture. "But couldn't I do that *with* Tony?"

"You'll make a better deal if you do it on your

own. Then they'll think they owe you something. Otherwise, Tony will be the one they concentrate on. And the one they'll primarily protect."

As Max took this in, he felt a gradual easing of his apprehension. Bogardus now seemed like a nurse, a very stiff and starched but wholly dependable and quite comfortable nurse, who was turning down the corner of a spotless bed and telling him to take off his clothes, his worries, his fears, to get in and sleep the sleep of reassurance and peace. A dull reassurance, a dull peace, perhaps, but no less desirable for being that. And Max, closing his eyes, knowing that the nurse would understand his silence, allowed himself to assess just how weary he was. He thought of Elaine and her spitefulness, of his daughters and their jeeriness; he thought of Tony and his hideous betrayal; he thought of Lassatta and death. Bogardus was right. There had to be an end to running. Yet when he spoke, it was not immediately to accept the plan.

"What's there in it for you?" he demanded bluntly. "Tony still goes to jail. As a matter of fact, it's worse for him. He loses his chance to make a deal for himself."

"Exactly." For the first time there was the hint of a glitter in those kindly eyes. "And that is what there's in it for me. You can imagine what a father-in-law must think of a son-in-law like Tony. All I want to do is rescue my daughter and her children. If he makes a public confession and traps some big criminals, he may become a kind of hero. I know Lee. It will appeal to the romantic in her. But if he's trapped himself by your confession, he's just another rat. It's harder for her to glamorize it."

Max shrugged. "She still may."

"Oh, I know. But it gives me a chance."

Max laughed nastily. "Come on, Bogardus. Admit it. It gives *you* a chance. To deprive Tony of his big moment. Because you hate his guts!"

Bogardus rose and nodded his head toward the door. "I guess our interview is over, Mr. Leonard."

8

Central Park had come to be for Tony a symbol of release from his tensions. He walked there in the early morning when he couldn't sleep and again in the late afternoon, before coming home. It was early spring and damp, and the city that formed the concrete oblong frame to this blessed patch of green might have been all the sins of the universe pressed about a single soul. But here, in the middle of that frame, strolling in the Mall, sitting on a bench by a lake, he could breathe.

Each day of the week that he had decided to give Max to make up his mind had been tenser than the one before. The state of euphoria into which he and Lee had entered, the burst of their first enthusiasm, had not lasted. He was still convinced that he had to do what he was going to do, but Lee had become the prey of inevitable doubts. Her nervousness was now pitiable. They had agreed not to discuss the matter, but as no other topic was possible, their evenings had been full of wretched silences. Lee would stare at the children with eyes of painful doubt and apprehension, so that even Isabel had begun to ask her what was wrong. Tony yearned to have it all over. He was afraid of giving in to Lee's implied appeal. He was afraid of going back to the old state.

On Thursday morning, walking in the Mall, just as he was beginning to convince himself that he was not bound to Max by his own unilateral decision to wait a full week, he became conscious of a man on a bench who was looking at him. He was a young man, in a light suit with a pink tie, and very thick blond hair. He got up now and walked beside Tony.

"Keep walking," he muttered. "Lassatta sent me."

Tony stopped immediately and faced him. "I don't care to keep walking," he said coldly. "If you have something to tell me, tell me."

The man's eyes moved from side to side.

"Your pal Leonard's gone to the police. He's blabbed his story and asked for protection. They got him hid away already."

"How do you know?"

"*I* don't know. Lassatta knows. It happened last night. The word to you is keep cool. Deny everything. They can't prove anything through Leonard. The meetings, the money, they were all part of a political deal."

"Why were they secret then?"

"You couldn't afford to be connected with Lassatta. It fits like a glove."

Tony frowned. It did fit. For what could the government prove about Menzies, Lippard? To do nothing was what he had been bribed to do, and nothing was exactly what he had done. It was

Max's word against his, and he knew which would be the better witness.

"I see," he said. "It fits."

"I can tell Lassatta you'll go along?"

Tony shook his head. "You can tell Lassatta I shall do precisely as I think best."

The man's face quickly lost all expression. "Better be careful, pal."

"I *shall* be careful."

"You could get hurt. Very hurt."

"So could others."

"You got two kids. Just remember that."

Tony felt the tips of his fingers tingle. He had a vision of his hands moving, independently of himself, like two flying things, two bats, and fixing themselves murderously around this little man's pudgy neck. He closed his eyes and breathed deeply to push away the image. It would be such ecstasy to kill.

"Scram," he muttered.

"Just remember what I say, pal. Just remember those kids. Nobody's asking you to do anything but save your goddam neck."

"You can tell Lassatta you have delivered your message," Tony said and, turning abruptly, he walked away. He wondered, almost without interest, if the man would shoot.

He decided to go back to the apartment. Lee would be startled, thinking he had gone downtown. He paused before his front door to look at his watch. Eight-thirty. The children would have left for school. From inside he could hear the sound of the vacuum cleaner. He rang the bell, and it stopped. Lee opened the door and stared in astonishment.

"Did you forget your key?" she asked. "What are you home for?" When he did not answer, she took in what must have been his ghastly pallor for she cried out: "Oh, Tony, something's wrong!"

"Perhaps. I'm not exactly sure." He came in quickly and closed the door. "Max has gone to the police. Or the U. S. Attorney. He's told everything."

Lee's eyes closed. "Oh, God," she whispered. "Why?"

"He's scared to death. He wants to be protected."

"From whom?"

"From the bad guys."

"And you? How does it leave you?"

"Presumably I'll be arrested."

"Oh, Tony, how sordid!" She gave a little groan. "And the other way would have been so *fine*."

They sat in the living room, and he told her of his talk in the park, everything but the threat of the children. She followed him intently, with great, worried eyes.

"But this puts an entirely different complexion on things!" she exclaimed.

"I don't see why."

"That man in the park is perfectly right. You must deny everything. You can't let that sniveling little Max get away with this. Now you'll have to admit I was right about him. Let's leave him with his horrid little lie smeared all over his nasty face."

"Lie?"

"Well, it *will* be a lie, the way he'll tell it. Because nobody will ever give you the credit of having meant to confess. You'll appear not only guilty but stupid. Oh, darling, I can't stand it! We'll have the rest of our lives to be good in, but don't let

Max smear you with this. It's your *duty* to fight it. Your duty to Eric and Isabel."

"My duty to give perjured testimony?"

"Oh, don't use legal terms on me. We're beyond that. Think of the effect on Eric. You and I agreed that the only way to get him through this thing was to convince him you'd redeemed yourself by going to the authorities and coming clean. We thought he might even come to admire you for it. But *this* way! Oh, no, Tony. It won't do."

Tony rose and walked to the fireplace. "Do you really propose, Lee, that I get up in court and brand Max as a liar? That I ally myself with men like Lassatta and Menzies?"

"If it'll work, yes. Oh, Tony, *listen* to me." She followed him about the room now, making her appeal in clipped, tense syllables. "I know you think I'm a cynic, but I'm not. It's a maneuver, that's all. To gain time till you can find a better ground to take a stand on. You keep Max from destroying you and your family. Which is what he's after, believe me. You haven't got the moral right to destroy your capacity to do good. To make yourself contemptible to your own children!"

"You listen to me now, Lee. Believe me, love, I know what I'm doing. And I know what the risks are. I think I'm almost glad it's too late for me to confess. There's something so boy scout and cheap movie about striding up to an officer and saying: 'Take me. I did it. With my little hatchet!' It's a cleaner, sounder business to be caught. Caught red-handed. Then there's no nonsense about being a pompous ass. Everything is simplified. I did wrong. I got caught. I went to jail. Try to forgive me, if I prefer it this way."

Lee covered her face and sobbed violently. "I might. If you had mentioned me and the children once in that prosy sermon. Just once! But there's no room for us in your masturbatory romance."

Everything seemed to go out inside Tony at this. His heart was as cold as a sunless, unpeopled world, a vision of dark and icy night. "Help me, Lee, can't you?" he begged. "I don't know if I can get through this without you."

"Oh, yes, you can!" she cried furiously. "You can perform to a grandstand of Tony Lowders." As she looked up at him, her eyes narrowed. "That man in the park? Did he threaten you?"

"They always do."

"But he did?"

"Yes."

"And the children, what about them? Did he threaten them?"

Tony hesitated. "Yes."

"Oh, *Tony!*"

"But it's only bluff you know. They never take it out on children. Anyway, you'll have police protection."

Lee's drawn face seemed to show that she was divided between incredulity and renewed outrage. "You mean," she half-whispered, "you'll actually risk the lives of your children—never mind about mine—I know you don't care about that—but you'll actually risk the lives of Eric and Isabel, rather than let Max down?"

"Rather than lie. Rather than save Lassatta and Menzies. Rather than play their vicious game. It's got to stop somewhere, Lee."

"But why do *my* children have to pay for it?" Lee was approaching hysteria. "My poor innocent babes? Damn you, Tony Lowder, must we all perish to swell your ego?"

"Please, Lee." But her violence was helping him. He thought he saw his way through now. That icy darkness would not have to last. "You and the children will be *all right.*"

"You're a monster!" Her face seemed to crumple up, and she turned away. "I'm a fool to plead with you. Nothing makes a dent on you."

"I can do what I'm doing and still love you."

"Go to hell, will you? Will you please go to hell!"

"I've already been there," he said, and caught her hands as she jumped up and started pounding his chest.

9

Lee sometimes felt that she—or the incidence of marriage—had interrupted the central progress of Tony's development. It was not that she was under any illusion that she had dominated him. But she wondered if the husband of her middle years had not lost some of the incisiveness of action of the younger man to whom she had engaged herself. It was as if marriage had been a kind of roadblock which had split up the oncoming force of Tony Lowder, so that part of it had had to go around, part to slip over the top, part even to seep or tunnel under. The force had all got past, one way or another, but it had shown up on the other side in plural form. Tony's activities were now smaller versions of what she fancied had been previously a central drive, some philanthropic, some sentimental, some perhaps purely selfish. The different Tonys to whom she thus found herself married: the Tony who cared about the neighborhood poor, the Tony who fussed over his relatives, the Tony who went into speculative and unsuccessful ventures with Max Leonard, the Tony who spent hours talking with Joan Conway, were all different in their attitudes to Lee.

"If I had been a strong woman like Joan, you'd never have married me," she told him once, in their early years.

"Joan's not as strong as she looks."

"I'll buy that. What I meant was that if I'd *looked* as strong as Joan, you'd never have married me."

"I can't imagine your looking as strong as Joan."

"Exactly!"

"But whatever you'd looked like, darling, you'd have surely been. And it might have been terrible to *be* as strong as Joan looks. Anyway, you wouldn't have been Lee Bogardus, so how could I have married you?"

"Are you glad you did?"

"Silly."

"What have I really ever done for you?"

"You mean that Joan couldn't have done?"

"Exactly!" she cried again.

He paused, trying for her sake to be serious. "You've turned me back into a feeling person."

"Back?"

"Well, I'd been one as a boy. At least I think so."

"And you stopped being one?"

"Oh for years."

"Are you sure it was a good thing to go back? Maybe you had it made."

"I wasn't living."

Well, it was all very well to have this kind of talk in the first two years of marriage when one did not basically believe that anything could go wrong with love. She and Tony could risk any questions and almost any speculations. But when she had been married five years and caught him for the first time in a premeditated lie, her whole life seemed to fall apart.

She had taken Isabel and Eric to Narragansett to spend July with her parents in their big, old, weatherbeaten shingle cottage on the beach. Tony was to come for weekends. She hated leaving him, but she wanted to get the children out of town, and they were both anxious to save the summer rental. She made a point of calling Tony every day in the late afternoon. One night, however, when he had told her that he would be working late and she was feeling particularly lonesome, she called his office at nine o'clock. Another lawyer answered the telephone and told her that Tony had left at six. Taking in her concern, he obligingly looked about the mail desk and discovered a note from Tony directing that a printer's proof be delivered to the doorman at 771 Park Avenue and held for Mr. Lowder. Lee knew the number to be that of the Conways' apartment house. She was too proud to call there, but she called her own apartment every hour without an answer until four in the morning, when she fell asleep, exhausted and sobbing.

At nine-fifteen she telephoned Tony at his office and asked him why he had not answered.

"I must have slept through your rings," he explained casually. "Or else you were calling a wrong number."

"Or else you weren't there!"

There was a pause. "Where would I have been?"

"You tell me."

"Sweetie, your *tone!*"

"Never mind my tone. You spent the night at Joan Conway's!"

"How do you deduce that?"

"Well, can you deny it?"

"Would you believe me if I did?"

"Oh, Tony, at least *say* you weren't!" she almost shouted.

"*Why?* You're going to believe what you want, anyway."

"Then don't bother to come up this weekend!"

"Very well."

"Or any weekend!"

"Have a nice summer."

She slammed down the receiver and again burst into tears. Was it really possible that a marriage could end in two minutes? Were they now what was called "separated"?

She hurried to her mother's bedroom and found Selena, as usual at that hour, seated at the big, all-mirror dressing table, covered with aids to beauty, brushing her golden hair and rubbing cold cream into her lineless cheeks. Selena knew that people marveled at the finished product, and she delighted at their marveling. No matter that the product was artificial. What otherwise would there have been to admire?

"I've just discovered that Tony spent last night with Joan Conway!"

Selena was working on the circles under her eyes, and she did not speak for a minute. "Was Mr. Conway there?"

"How could he have been? We saw him last night, don't you remember? At the Talbots', for cocktails? He's on that cruise."

"Oh, yes. And she wasn't at the Talbots', was she?"

"No. She wasn't."

Selena now reached for a tissue and started to remove some of the cream. "Well, that's what you get for leaving him."

"Leaving him! You mean it's unreasonable to trust a husband from Monday to Friday?"

"In your case, I guess it must be."

"Oh, Mummie! You sound as if this were something of no importance!"

"It's exactly what you make of it, dear heart." Selena made the most extraordinary contortion to reach a spot below a nostril. "Some men are like cows that have to be regularly milked. Personally, I find it distasteful, but I suppose it's not their fault. A loving and faithful wife is thrown away on them." Selena's approving eyes seemed to congratulate her image for not trying to appeal to the coarser sex.

"You think I should put up with this?"

"Well, I don't say you shouldn't give him hell. I think you should. It was indiscreet of him, to say the least, to get caught. Supposing Mr. Conway finds out? He struck me as a rather violent man."

"Maybe he doesn't care," Lee said sullenly.

"How did you catch Tony?"

"I didn't really. I mean I haven't any proof."

"Then I wouldn't go looking for any."

Lee now went to her father's study. He was reading the newspaper and smiled in the particularly amiable way that he had when he most hated to be interrupted. As she told her tale, however, she was surprised at how quickly he, too, accepted the situation. Indeed, the lecture that he proceeded to deliver might have been prepared in advance for just this occasion.

"There's something you and I never went into, Lee, at the time you were married, and that is the difference in Tony's background and yours. I knew you'd flare right up, like all of your generation, if I so much as mentioned it, so I kept my mouth shut. Oh, I'm no fool. Besides, these differences don't matter so much any more, and I was and am very fond of Tony. But you have to understand that to a man of Tony's origins a woman like Mrs. Norris Conway is going to appear a very different creature than she appears to you. You have been brought up to take wealth and social position in your stride, and you assume that Tony is going to do the same. You couldn't be more wrong. To Tony she is a kind of queen, or golden goddess. To enjoy the favors of a woman like that is not simply a matter of sex. It's the fulfillment of an ambition—a sort of scaling the Matterhorn, if you want to put it that way ..."

Lee was too astonished even to laugh. That her father, who never showed the smallest interest in society or its doings, who hardly ever went out, except to a few neighbors' houses, should attribute such force to the powers of snobbishness seemed to indicate that she had never understood him.

"I'll try to see it in that light," she murmured and almost stumbled out of the house in her need to be alone. On the beach she fell on her knees and scooped up the sand desperately with both hands. She had a dismal notion that she had soiled, not her marriage (for what had that become?) but her ideal of it. She had made herself and Tony, by even discussing the matter, as sordid as her parents saw them. She got up to run—actually to run, so bad was the pain—when she saw a large man in a red sweater and white shorts walking swiftly down the beach toward her.

It was Norry Conway.

Later she was to remember with surprise how quickly she reasserted control of herself. Perhaps, after all, she was a woman made for crises. Norry did not even greet her. He sat down by her on the sand, hugging his knees and staring out to sea.

"I've been debating all night whether I should come here, and I finally decided I had to. Tell me something, for God's sake, Lee. What are our spouses to each other?"

The small, almost affected laugh that she managed reminded her of her mother. "Some people might pretend to be surprised by such a question. But I think it's entirely natural. Joan and Tony are simply the most tremendous friends."

"What does that mean?"

"I don't know exactly, but I know what it doesn't mean. It doesn't mean they're lovers."

She was even able to face calmly his angry stare.

"How do you know?"

"Because I *do* know. Because I should know it with everything in me if Tony was unfaithful."

"You really believe that?"

"Totally."

Norris was more than taken aback. He was actually embarrassed. "I'm sorry," he muttered.

"You needn't be. Joan and Tony have something to give each other, but it's not their bodies. They have a kind of tense understanding which may be for their mutual benefit. I know it's frustrating and infuriating for you. Oh, believe me, I know! But you and I should try to be big about it. It's the only way. Marriage is not the total possession of another person. It can't be, and it shouldn't be."

As she took in the relaxation of his heavy, puffy face and sensed the easing of that large, threatening frame, she saw that she had succeeded. Norris might take her for a trusting idiot, a prosy ass, but he was over the crisis. In one morning she had lost and saved her marriage. For it was perfectly clear to her now as she laughed a bit giddily and looked over the green tossing ocean that she was going to accept what she had. Somehow, miraculously, Norris Conway had seemed to create her solution. She had come out of the isolation of her dreams and had performed an act, a solid act, here, on this sandy earth. She would be able to live again so long as Tony never tried to take her back to the unbelievable bliss of their honeymoon.

Part III

1

Tony sat at the U. S. Attorney's table in the District Courtroom at Foley Square. The dying sunlight of the early winter afternoon flickered against the high window through which he could see only a gray, cloudless sky. His glance circled the bare walls of the clean, austere chamber and dropped to the packed rows of quiet, listening spectators behind the rail. Mr. Lanigan, Menzies' lawyer, was arguing an objection. The jurors made no effort to conceal their boredom at this legal interruption of the drama. Judge Fenton, whose long cerebral face seemed pulled into a kind of fixed attention, stared at Lanigan with empty eyes.

"But I submit again, Your Honor, that it bears on the all vital question of the credibility of the witness Lowder. Lowder has already been indicted and convicted for the same crime of conspiracy to break a federal law with which the defendants Lassatta and Menzies stand here charged. Lowder had no trial, for he pleaded guilty. He has not been sentenced, or even incarcerated, pending the results of this proceeding. In other words, Uncle Sam, Lowder's stern but potentially benevolent relative, is looking down to see how well he testifies here. And Lowder knows and I know, and Your Honor knows, and this jury knows—indeed this whole courtroom knows—that the length of Lowder's sentence will depend on the exact degree of his cooperation with the federal prosecuting authorities!"

"Mr. Lanigan," the Judge interrupted, "you have made that argument a dozen times in this trial, and it has been repeatedly ruled on."

"It cannot be made too often, Your Honor!"

"I say it can. You have ample exceptions for any appeal you may wish to make. Let us get on with the testimony."

Mr. Lanigan suffered from the kind of bumpy, ill-shaped stoutness that puts to rout the stiffest, most determined clothes. No belt could hold his shirt down, no garter his socks up; no pin could fasten the edges of his collar. Yet he seemed to live in a kind of nervous frenzy, refusing to accept this fact. He was constantly pressing down his tumbling, greasy hair and pushing back the glasses that slipped over his snubby nose. Such frenzy, however, was not altogether against him as an advocate. It somehow intensified the sincerity of his large, unhappy eyes. Jack Eldon, the Assistant U.S. Attorney, had told Tony that Lanigan was not a regular criminal lawyer. It was probably why he was so nasty.

"I wish to recall the Special Assistant to the Regional Director," Lanigan said, turning toward Tony.

Tony resumed the seat that he had already occupied for long days of questioning. He knew now that he could go on as long as need be, answering the same kinds of questions in the same kind of monotone, indifferent to Lanigan's efforts to anger him, until the exhausted jury should accept the simple fact that he was speaking the truth.

"Perhaps, Mr. Lowder, I should no longer refer to you as the Special Assistant to the Regional Director?"

"It's hardly accurate. I resigned the position months ago."

"Resigned?"

"Yes, Mr. Lanigan, resigned. I would have been fired if I hadn't, of course, but it is technically still correct to say that I resigned."

"Does it pain you to be addressed by that title?"

"Not in the least."

"But you would rather I call you simply by your name?"

"Call me Butch, if you want."

"Ah, but I don't want. I don't want to at all. Would you tell me, Mr. Lowder, just how long you had occupied the position of Special Assistant to the Regional Director when you decided to accept this alleged bribe from the defendants?"

"Between one and two months. Nearer two, I think."

"You mean as Hamlet said of his mother's remarriage: 'Nay, not so much, not two'?" Mr. Lanigan smiled at the jury to apologize for his erudition and to assure them that he knew they recognized his quotation. "And prior to your taking this position as Special Assistant, had you ever occupied a federal office?"

"Never."

"Nor a state one?"

"No."

"Or city?"

"No, I'd never previously occupied any government position."

"And yet, less than eight short weeks after taking your first oath of public office, you were looking about to see how best to line your pockets? Or had you, indeed, taken the post in the expectation of just such extra emoluments?"

"Your Honor," Jack Eldon protested, rising, "I submit that Mr. Lanigan is harassing the witness. He has established over and over again that Mr. Lowder accepted a bribe. Nor did he have to, for Mr. Lowder pleaded guilty to the charge. What is to be gained by rubbing it in?"

"I agree with you, Mr. Eldon," the Judge replied. "I was about to intervene myself. I should have done so earlier had it not been perfectly evident that Mr. Lowder was not in the least bothered by these pin pricks. I must insist, Mr. Lanigan, that you have already covered this ground, unless you can persuade me that you have a new point to make."

When the Court, shortly after this, adjourned for ten minutes, Jack Eldon surprised Tony by walking after him to the corridor and offering him a cigarette. They had come to know each other very well during the trial and in its preparation, but never before had Jack shown the least interest in a personal relationship. Indeed, his polite formality had suggested that he held Tony in the greatest contempt, as a traitor, not only to the legal profession, but to the greater world of "gentlemen." Eldon, a tense, pale, rather beautiful man in his early thirties, with glittering eyes and tumbling, curly black hair, was a graduate of Groton and Harvard. He had taken a leave of absence from the great Wall Street firm of which he was a junior partner to act as Assistant U. S. Attorney out of a sheer sense of public duty. He was in many ways an anachronism, and by Tony's lights, a bit of a Parsifal, but he was attractive and brilliant. He had handled the trial with the skill of an old prosecutor. It had been a triumph of brains over experience.

"Has anyone discovered your new telephone number yet?" he asked Tony.

"No, my evenings are blissfully silent. No crank calls. No calls of any sort."

"You're still sure you wouldn't care to go into protective custody? We'd prefer it, you know."

"No, I like my empty apartment. I'm grateful to be out on bail. I don't really think anybody's going to take a shot at me, and if they do . . . well, think of the problems *that* would solve."

But Eldon did not want to think of them. He turned away, embarrassed, from Tony's easy smile. "I wish you'd stay more in that apartment. These weekend bicycle rides of yours are very tempting to Mafiosi. Last Sunday we followed you all the way to Coney Island. My poor agent was exhausted."

"So that's who he was. I thought as much. I'm sorry, but I can't give up my rides. Think how soon I won't be able to go anywhere!" Tony now realized that he liked to be talking again. He inhaled the cigarette deeply and became almost lyrical. "You ought to try bicycling, Jack. All through Central Park, very fast, very green, with its mountain range of towers. And Prospect, with its jungles of plants. Even Queens, with its desert wastes. And along the Sound, with those huge bridges. It's the only way to take in New York—for better or worse. In the automobile you're an invader. On foot, you're a victim. But on a bicycle . . . well, you're with the city, of the city. I live again, if it is living. I'm even happy."

Eldon looked at him with undisguised curiosity. "What do you hear from your family?"

"Nothing. I don't even know where they are. My father-in-law has hidden them away in the country."

"Well, of course, I know that."

Tony paused to give this proper consideration. It seemed so odd that this young man should know where his family was and that he should not. "Is it a safe place?"

Eldon shrugged. "I guess so. But we don't really think they're in any danger. I believe there's no case on record of the Mafia taking it out on a wife and children."

"Well, I guess it's natural for my father-in-law to be nervous."

"Yes, but they could still call you."

"You don't get it, Jack." Tony was surprised that, knowing so much, Eldon did not know all. "Lee has left me."

People were returning to the courtroom already. Jack, suddenly flushing, clapped him on the shoulder. "Would you like to come for dinner tonight? Just Judith and me?"

Tony was too surprised to speak for a moment. "Well, sure, I guess. If you think it looks all right."

"I think it looks just fine. Seven?"

When the Court adjourned for the day, Tony

walked home. He did it every day, though it took him more than an hour, for it gave him exercise on the weekdays and helped him to sleep. Besides, there was nothing else to do. He could not read, and he found that movies acted on his nerves. There was nobody whom he could bear to see, except Joan, and her visitors were now restricted to a few minutes. He felt guilty about his mother, who was desolate over his refusal to spend his evenings with her, but her heavy sympathy and commiseration were intolerable. He needed to be alone to get to know the new Tony Lowder who was going to be his principal if not his only companion in the long aftermath.

It was difficult to be sure just what was happening to the inner Tony because the process of becoming a public criminal had such a stunning, doping effect on the imagination. It filled his mind to the exclusion of everything else. When he awoke in the morning, his first thought was: "Here's another day for Tony Lowder, convicted crook." Everything that happened to him: the rudeness of Lanigan, the jibes of the columnists who were as moral as nineteenth-century parsons, even his abandonment by Lee and her chilling silence seemed orderly and predictable parts of a perfectly understandable punishment. He was alone because he had taken himself out of his world. But he was not in agony, perhaps because he was still numb.

It was plain that one day the numbness was going to cease, and then he would presumably feel the full pain of losing his family. But it was also quite possible that he would get them back. He understood perfectly that the great danger of his situation was self-pity. He had ruined forever his career as a lawyer and politician. That was obvious enough. But he did not have to have ruined his private career. The difference was that whereas before there had been a noisy grandstand of friends and family to applaud success, or the appearance of it, or even to boo in a friendly way at failure, now there were only tiers of empty seats. What he had to do—if he was to avoid the bathos of despair—was to adapt himself to the changeover from a life where the thermometer of his actions had been provided by others to a life where it was provided by himself alone. But the point was—and he kept making it again and again as he trudged the blocks—that the business of living might still be amusing enough, even transacted with oneself. There were people whose favorite game was solitaire.

"Tony, old boy, how are you? Sorry for the trouble you're in. I always knew Max was a goddam sneak!"

It was a friend, a fellow lawyer, walking in the opposite direction at Eighteenth Street. Tony nodded, returned the hearty grip and walked on. There were those who avoided him, and those who, like this fellow, covered their embarrassment in heartiness. Nobody, of course, reviled him. Nobody stopped to tell him that he had kicked another hole in the collapsing wall of public confidence. But all reactions were becoming the same to him. The reactors were on one side of the fence; he on the other. It would take a lot more getting used to, but he was getting used to it.

"Is that you, Tony? Tony Lowder! Don't run off. I just want to tell you that you're doing a fabulous job of testifying against those goons . . ."

"They only did what I did," Tony muttered, and hurried on. This time the man was someone he did not know. His picture, of course, had been in all the papers and on television.

"Aren't you Tony Lowder?"

He nodded and passed on. Sometimes it was like that, three in two blocks. More often his evening journey was in peace. On foot or on bicycle he was able to continue the inner dialogue without interruption, to continue arranging and rearranging, like a puzzle of colored cubes, the few small pieces of his future. It sometimes seemed to him that the person with whom he discussed their arrangement was a being just other than himself, a slightly larger Tony Lowder who supervised the plight of the smaller one, the bigger Tony being presumably a figure into whom the smaller might be expected ultimately to grow. In much the same way, at Joan's Sunday lunch party, he had felt alone with respect to the other guests, but not with respect to this presence in himself. Was it grace?

"Was it God?"

He stopped and looked about. Nobody had spoken to him. His wince had not been at the comment of some passer-by, some possible witness to a chance exclamation uttered aloud by mistake. No, that wince had been one of simple shame at the idea that he should have called on God. To such a low rank had the deity been reduced in his subconscious.

He found himself thinking of Joan Conway and her old nurse, Annie, whom she had always kept with her. Annie had been hidden away behind the scenes, a smiling, illiterate, crooning old Irish woman, eternally knitting in Joan's boudoir where she could be available for her mistress' hugs, like an old rag doll. Annie, he supposed, had been Joan's God. Well, she had done as much for Joan as such a god could do. It was a pity she had not survived to see Joan through.

He was startled by the empty parlor into which the maid showed him. He had known that Jack Eldon was rich, but he had supposed that his riches would have expressed themselves more sternly, more traditionally, in Chippendale and porcelains of China trade and sporting prints. Instead, he found himself in a very feminine interior, made up at obvious expense and all at once by a fashionable decorator whose commission must have covered every last book and picture. If the husband was allowed to bring his pipe and newspaper into such a room, he might deem himself fortunate. The colors were loud but not strident, the abstracts gay and not grim; the table decorations were Arp-like sculptures converted to ashtrays. Beneath Tony's feet spread a huge rug representing a backgammon board. Through the open door to a seemingly all-glass dining room he was surprised to see a table set for some dozen people. The last thing that he had expected was a party! But when Judith Eldon came in, a little blonde slip of a thing in scanty, gauzelike pink, not more than twenty-one years old, he understood. She obviously belonged to the world of continous fete.

"Well, I've certainly heard a lot about *you*," she began. "It's high time Jack brought you home. I understand you bicycle around the city, careless of risk. And that you threatened Jack you wouldn't be as good a witness if they put you in protective custody. Is that true?"

"More or less." Tony liked her yellow eyes. They were large and cool and frank. "I induced your husband to see it my way."

"Aren't you afraid?"

"I don't think about it."

"Because you don't care. I see that. And, of course then, nothing will happen to you."

"It takes caring?"

"It takes caring. About a drink, for example." She moved over to the bar table. "You're not beyond that?"

"Oh, no."

She poured him his whiskey as he had asked for it, straight, and continued in her intimate vein. "Jack says your wife has left you. How mean of her. Doesn't she believe in what you're doing? Believe in your helping Jack? With all your wonderful testimony?"

Tony shook his head. "Oh, least of all that. She thinks that's the purest self-indulgence. At her expense. Most women would agree with her, don't you think? When a man leans more to a principle than to a woman, he's going to find himself in trouble with that woman. What else should he expect?"

"Well, he should expect his wife to know that's how men are," Judith retorted. "*I* know. Nobody could be married to Jack for a year and not know. He's all for moral principles. Why, his divorce from his first wife almost killed him!"

"Don't you believe in moral principles, Mrs. Eldon?"

"Call me Judy. No."

"Not any?"

"Well, I don't believe in them where individuals are concerned. For example, take you. I suppose I don't believe that government officials should take bribes. But the moment I meet you, you cease to be a government official. You become Tony Lowder. That's different."

"That's sentimental."

"But women *are* sentimental. So are men—the men of my generation, anyhow. Your wife wouldn't give a damn what you did if she thought you really loved her. You'll see. It'll be all right."

"Because I really do love her?"

Judith looked at him critically for a moment and then nodded. "Yes. I think you do."

Jack Eldon at this point came hurriedly into the room. He had just arrived from his office.

"Tony, I'm terribly sorry. I didn't realize, when I asked you, that Judith had friends for dinner. But it's all arranged. You and I will have our dinner in the library and shan't be disturbed at all."

Judith looked from one man to the other, smiling. "Maybe Tony would *like* to dine with us."

"Don't be ridiculous, Judith. It's out of the question. Do you want to embarrass him to death?"

"But, Jack," Tony interposed. "I can go. Your guests will need you."

"My guests? You mean Judith's. Certainly not. You will oblige us both very much if you do just as I say. Please bring your drink into the library."

Tony bowed to Judith and followed his host obediently into the small, paneled, book-filled room where Jack was evidently allowed to escape from the remorselessness of his wife's interior decoration. He noted, as Jack closed the door, that this room, too, had a bar table.

"I didn't know you'd been divorced," he said, while Jack was making his own drink. "You were so worked up about Lee."

"I learned the hard way."

"You mean your wife left you?"

Tony noted with composure how vividly he had discountenanced his host. Jack's lips tightened, and his pale face, which Tony could see in profile, seemed even paler. He took a deep swallow of his drink without turning around.

"No. I left her for Judith."

"Did you have children?"

"Oh, yes. Three. At the worst ages for that kind of thing, too. Twelve to seven. It was all pretty ghastly. I don't know why I'm telling you."

"Because I'm a convicted crook. Like a dead person. Perhaps I shouldn't be so personal, but the prospect of jail makes me impatient of small talk."

"Everyone was against me," Jack continued, as if he had not heard Tony. "They were all on Peggy's side. Even my parents. I was practically read out of the family. You'd think I'd invented divorce! You see, Peggy was so good and so wronged . . . God, it was hell!"

"I'm sure it was." Tony scrutinized his prosecutor's dark, shifting eyes. The latter had now taken a seat opposite him. "We don't need an after-life to balance old scores. But I have a kind of grudging admiration for a man who can break out of the kind of trap yours must have been."

"Even if he jumps into another?" Jack was surprised by the candor of his own question, for he followed it up with a quick, mirthless laugh.

"I couldn't have done it," Tony went on, ignoring this lead. "I could never bear to hurt people. That can be a terrible weakness, you know. When I was a boy, I went through the usual religious phase, but it all blew up when I read the history of religion. Nothing but crucifixions and burnings and throwing to wild beasts. I wanted no part of it. I still don't."

But Jack was not interested in religion. He was interested in cases, in his own and in Tony's. "There's something I've been wanting to ask you," he said now. "Something that's been puzzling me. Why are you being so cooperative in this case?"

"I should have thought you might have heard Mr. Lanigan answer that one often enough."

"Oh, to reduce your term, of course. But there's still something in the whole business I don't get. Maybe I should be asking why you did what you did, not why you're doing what you're doing."

"It might be more interesting."

"That's it. For you *are* interesting, Tony. I find myself thinking more and more what your motives can have been. At first I didn't like you at all."

"Oh, I knew that."

"Did I make it so obvious?"

"Not that obvious. But I could tell."

"And now I do like you. Very much. But I'm damned if I understand you."

Tony reflected on the peculiarity of his not even being tempted to tell Jack that he had been forestalled in his plan of confessing. He saw perfectly how completely it would rehabilitate him in Jack's mind, but this now seemed a matter of little importance. He did not feel the least compulsion to mitigate his crime in Jack's or anyone else's mind. What he had done was quite as wicked as any of them cared to think or not to think. The only thing that had happened to him that was in any way remarkable was the feeling that had come over him afterward, but this experience had been so intensely personal—so exclusively personal—that he knew that there was no point even trying to convey to another what it was like. Had he not tried with Lee? With her father?

"Well, I like you, Jack," he said, and he hoped that it did not sound perfunctory. "And I doubt if you're any easier to understand."

Jack raised his glass. "Good," he said. "We've got that settled. We like each other, and we're both very difficult to understand. Such interesting people! I drink to you, Tony, and to a suspended sentence. But whatever happens, remember this. You're not nearly as dead as you think."

2

Lee sat alone in her father's office, waiting for him to return. He had told her that he had to confer briefly with one of his partners who was going to Washington that afternoon, but she knew he had gone to the men's room. It was his time. Why did the neatness and bareness of his office strike her for the first time that day as pathetic? He did not *have* to have only one picture on the wall: a drawing of William Maxwell Evarts challenging the constitutionality of the income tax before the Supreme Court. His desk did not have to be stripped of all objects but the tiny bronze replica of Hudson's vessel, the *Half Moon*, and a silver-framed photograph of Selena, looking very regal (her mother's little private fantasy). And there was no necessity for the bookcase to be a stranger to all volumes but tax reporters and the Social Register. No, it was pathetic because it was like a monk's chamber. It was pathetic because there was so little consolation in a religion of tax avoidance.

There was no picture of her and Tony. There had been one, she was quite sure, beside that of her mother. And now it was gone. Obviously, her father could not bear to look at him. Could she blame him? Could she bear to herself? In the last days had she not even begun to speculate that she might at last learn to live without Tony? The long dull weeks in northern Connecticut, in the borrowed house of one of her father's clients, where she had read novels while Eric roamed the woods with a bird book and Isabel pounded the piano, had taught her that peace, a dead peace, might lie ahead. But she wondered if she could ever learn to live, not without Tony, but without her love of him. That, she was beginning to see, would be her real problem. She was more dependent on the habit than on the man.

She might have forgiven him but for Eric. It had been too terrible to watch the boy's silent suffering. He never complained about being out of school and never once mentioned Tony. But he had given up his old arguments with her and Isabel. It was only too evident that he felt disqualified, as the son of a dishonored man, to be the champion of law and order. When he talked it was all of particular things: birds he had seen, or trees, or the plots of novels he had read. But for the most part he was silent and moody.

Isabel, as Lee had foreseen, let it all out in emotional outbursts. She even seemed to enjoy the excitement of the isolation, the drama of the newspapers. At times her tears were genuine; at times, stagey. But she would come through. No thanks to Tony. Lee clenched her fists in anger as she thought how little Tony had given to her or the children. Joan had only to beckon. Max had only to weep. His old mother had only to wail. But his own family he took for granted. Because they were a part of himself? That, of course, would be his argument. But if he thought so little of himself, it was hardly a compliment. It was certainly not enough of a compliment to live on.

The door opened and quickly closed, and her father was in the room, rubbing his hands. "There, my dear, there. I'm all ready for you now and our little discussion. Let me see. Let me see."

Lee watched as he folded his handkerchief twice and tucked it into his pocket, as he polished the lenses of his glasses and pushed the model of the *Half Moon* to and fro. It would be the same later, if he took her to lunch. He would straighten the silver, fuss with his napkin, nurse his food into yummy little particles, chew and chew, cough and blink, shift his buttocks over the seat. It was as if the sensuousness of some lost lover within him had been converted to a hundred nervous reflexes. What room could there be, in the heart of a man so absorbed, for a mere daughter?

"Your mother and I have exhaustively discussed our long-range plans," he was saying. "Let me assure you at once that we have agreed to take on the education of Eric and Isabel. It's a big tab to pick up, but, after all, they're our only grandchildren. We have decided to see them through."

"That's very generous, Daddy."

"Wait, my dear." His voice was always particularly gentle when he had something disagreeable to say. "There is a condition."

"A condition?" Lee demanded, instantly resentful. "Why should there be a condition? You and

Mummie are perfectly well off. You're rich—by my standards, anyway." She noted how he winced at the imputation. "I may be down and out, but I'm damned if I'll beg."

"I'm not going to ask you to beg," her imperturbable parent rejoined. "Eric and Isabel are my grandchildren, and I always expected to be a dutiful and loving grandparent. But you have suggested something quite different: namely that I assume the duties of a parent."

"Oh, I'll be around to do all the chores, don't worry."

"You evade me, darling. I am speaking of the financial duties of a parent. Those are the ones you wish me to assume, are they not?"

"Of course. What else?"

"Very well. And in assuming these duties—ones not normally required of a grandparent—I feel that I am entitled to stipulate a condition."

"Well, what is it?"

"I want you to divorce Tony." The words fell like a scythe on soft grass. "I want you to obtain custody of the children. I don't think that's unreasonable. Particularly as my firm will handle the details. I anticipate no trouble from Tony. I think he will understand that the smaller the role he plays in your lives, the better for all."

"Have you discussed this with him?"

"No."

Lee was startled to find that her first violent reaction was one of almost painful relief. Tony, at least, had not agreed to be abandoned. Then she reflected that her father was probably right. Tony would agree to it. He would claim that he was doing it as a necessary sacrifice. But would he be?

She stamped her foot under the desk. Was it another fagot in the pyre of his self-immolation?

"I think this may be very hard on Tony," she murmured, in the frustration of her conflict.

"It's entirely his doing. He has put you in a position where you can't practically do anything else. I suggest it's your simple duty to your children."

"What about my simple duty to my husband?"

"He's canceled it! He's released you from your vows! First, by his flagrant infidelity with Mrs. Conway. Secondly, by his crime in betraying a public trust. And lastly, and worst of all, by exposing you and the children to mortal danger with his reckless game of playing informer."

"You don't think that was his duty? To the public?"

"I think his first duty was to the home that he had violated and endangered."

Lee found that she was fighting for time. "Even if that were so," she pointed out, "haven't we to consider what people will think? I mean from the children's point of view. Will it be good for them to be known as having repudiated their father when he was in trouble?"

"It will have been done when they were young. You and I will take responsibility for that. They'll never be blamed."

"You assume, then, that *I* won't mind."

"Consider your dignity, Lee! This man has made hash out of your life. Oh, I know a lot of sentimental fools would clap their hands and toss their bonnets in the air if you 'stuck by him,' as they say. But you and I are not people to be swayed by the mob. We have standards, and we live up to them. And when a man breaks every trust, as Tony has, we should not be afraid to condemn him and cast him out! Particularly now that he seems to have developed messianic delusions! I propose that you take back your maiden name and call yourself Mrs. Lee Bogardus."

Lee frowned. "The children too?"

"The children too. That, however, is only a suggestion. It is not part of my condition."

She had not been prepared for the pitch of her father's resentment. Just as a neat housekeeper, forever emptying a single ash from an ashtray into a wastebasket lined with a plastic bag, would abominate a man who tossed his ashes on the rug, so did Pieter abominate the son-in-law who strewed the Bogardus life with crowd-attracting, derision-attracting filth.

"I guess he's not as bad as you think," she muttered.

Her father exploded. "What is there to be said in his behalf? What did we ever ask of him? Did we object to his shabby background and poor prospects? Was there any necessity for him to turn to crime? And when he *did* turn to it, did he have to muck it up so that he was not only caught but his family jeopardized? Oh, Lee, my dear child, you must face the fact that this man is not only totally egocentric, totally dishonest, but totally incompetent. He's a menace! We've got to have the courage of our convictions."

"But what are my convictions?" Lee looked hopelessely up at William Maxwell Evarts denouncing the iniquities of a graduated tax. "I don't really resent Tony's taking that bribe. Of course, I think he was a bloody idiot, but that's another matter. What I really resent is his turning into somebody different from the man I married. I used to get along by loving Tony. He didn't have to do anything much in return. He could worry about his lame ducks and fuss over his dreary parents and even go to bed with women whom he fancied that would somehow help. Because I, too, was a kind of lame duck. And as long as I was that, I would always own a small part of him. But then he had to go and take that bit away!"

Her father blinked at her, having taken little of this in. "Well, there you are, my dear. I don't think we're so very far apart."

Were they not? As she met his eyes, she felt the full impact of this second rejection. For had she not always taken it for granted that in the long run she was bound to prevail in any argument with her parents about her own welfare? Now she was brought up to a tight halt before the humiliating fact that her father's anger at Tony was greater than his love of her.

"We may be together, Daddy, but what good does that do me? Any decision about the future is a matter for the children."

"You don't mean you'd go back to him!"

"I might if I thought it were the right thing for Eric and Isabel." She paused, shocked by the hostility in those eyes. Did *he* feel rejected, too? "Oh, Daddy, why must you hate Tony so?"

"How can I not hate him? A man who talks about Christ in the Down Town Association!"

Lee found what relief she could in the one and only laugh that the morning had offered her. "Well, that *is* going pretty far, I admit."

••

Later that afternoon she called on Tony's parents. It was a family conference. Tony's sister Susan had come up from her office to meet her, and even his brother Philip was there, looking a strange caricature of Tony, wide and soft and greasy haired, with the bland, blue look of sustained bad temper. Tony's father, George, much deteriorated, watched a Western on television in the corner with the sound turned off.

"I know this will surprise you all," Dorothy Lowder was saying. "A reporter from the *News* is coming in to see me. He wants to hear my version of why Tony did what he did. I said I'd be proud to see him!"

"Oh, Mother, don't you think we should leave that kind of thing to Lee?"

"I do not, Susan." Dorothy looked defiantly at her daughter-in-law, who transferred her own gaze to the carpet. "Lee has chosen to be silent during this whole tragedy. She even went into hiding. All that is her affair, and I do not presume to criticize. But Tony's mother has a part of him, too. And I want to make it clear to all the world that I stand behind Tony to the very end. That I regard him as a hero."

"A hero!" Philip exclaimed with a hoot of jeering laughter. "Oh, Mom, come off it!"

"I do, Philip. I don't know how Tony became involved with these criminal types, but I have a strong suspicion that it may have been with the knowledge of the police."

"You mean that he was an informer from the start?" Philip cried sarcastically. "It seems rather tough that they'd convict him for it. Isn't that carrying their realism a bit far?"

"The police may have betrayed him, Philip."

Philip turned to Susan with a face pinched with exasperation. "Can favoritism go further?" he cried. "All my life I'm made to play second fiddle to Tony, and even now that he's a crook, he's still a hero."

"Well, I think he *is* a hero," Susan snapped, hurrying to repudiate her would-be ally. "I think he's a hero in the way he's taken the whole thing. He has given us all an unforgettable example of how to behave in adversity."

"I'm sorry I don't go in for that kind of cant," Philip sneered. "And I fail to see how you and Mother survive with your heads in that cloud of goo. If Tony's a hero, it's because he's been honest. Because he's dared to take a calculated risk for his own advancement. Oh, sure, he lost. In his game you've got to win. Now all the hypocrites and bureaucrats can point the finger of shame at him. But not his kid brother. *I* recognize the honest man in the striped suit. The only suit an honest man can wear in our putrid society."

"Oh, Philip, shut up!" his mother exclaimed indignantly. "Everything you say is just for effect."

Lee saw that they had all been exhilarated by Tony's fate. Their lives resembled some drought-stricken land, with dried-up creeks and empty ponds, with acres of cracked, hard mud under a darkening sky torn by intermittent rumbles of an ineffective thunder. And then, at last, the rain so long and vainly promised had come in the form of Tony's crime and punishment and had drenched the countryside and filled all the cracks and crannies with its life-reviving deluge. Dorothy, Philip and Susan had run out of the caves of their boredom and now raised their bare arms to the tempest, giggling and crying and splashing themselves.

Lee rose to go. "I'm glad you're all sticking by Tony," she said in a flat voice. "It will make it easier if I decide to divorce him."

"Lee!" Dorothy shrieked. "You can't!"

"Oh, why do you pretend to care, Mrs. Lowder? You'll have him all to yourself. He can live with you when he gets out."

"Lee, that's a rotten thing to say to Mother!" Susan exclaimed with sudden filial fervor.

"Oh, can't you all see I don't *care!*" Lee strode past the three of them, silent now before her unexpected violence, to speak to her father-in-law. He looked up at her with a vacant smile.

"Tony and Phil are just alike," he said in a reedy voice. "And just like their maternal grandfather."

"And you," Lee whispered in a sudden fit of disgust, "are the worst of all!"

But she was not to escape so easily. Despite her rebuff Dorothy Lowder followed her daughter-in-law doggedly out to the hall and pleaded with her to come into her bedroom for a private talk.

"Oh, Lee, they all hate me," she wailed, as soon as they were alone there. "Everyone but Tony detests me. You do. Oh, don't deny it! You always have. Why shouldn't you? What have I done to make you feel otherwise? But, don't you see, one can be a selfish, self-centered, obstinate old woman with nothing ahead but the grave and still want to be something better? Philip is so awful. He thinks anyone's a fool who tries to be better than they are. He sneers and jeers and thinks there's some kind of virtue in that. But where has it got him? And who is he to be so sure there's no place to get? Why should I be more convinced by Philip than by what I think myself?"

As Lee took in the ravaged look of those haunted pale eyes, she wondered if she could take on this problem, too. "But there's no reason," she assured Dorothy in a kinder tone. "No reason at all. Phil is a terrible ass. Everyone knows that."

"He is, isn't he?" Dorothy agreed eagerly, as if her second son had received a compliment. "Sometimes I think he and Susan are actually afraid I might have some satisfaction in life that I don't deserve."

"Don't deserve?"

"Well, they blame me, of course, because they're not happy. They don't want me to be happy, either. It's only natural. And, God knows, I haven't been happy. But there's no reason I shouldn't find *something* in life, is there?"

"Like what?" Lee wondered if Mrs. Lowder, for once, might not actually be trying to communicate a thought rather than an emotion.

"Like peace of mind. Or hope. Or faith."

"Faith?"

"Faith in God." The big worried eyes rolled and blinked and seemed not to see Lee. "Faith in God who punished my son for what he did and made him do what he's now doing."

Lee stared fixedly at her mother-in-law as she felt herself chilly all over. For Dorothy Lowder seemed to have forgotten that she was talking to her son's wife. She was completely obsessed with herself and her own problems, as usual, but there was now a marked difference. She was no longer interested in Lee's approval or pity, nor in the impression, good or bad, that she made on her. She was still taken up with Dorothy Lowder, of course, but now she was taken up with Dorothy Lowder and God. Even with Dorothy Lowder, a handful of dust, and God.

"Tony told you that?"

"Of course, he told me that. Just the way he told you that." Dorothy seemed suddenly peevish. "He came to see me the day before his trial started. Oh, he didn't put it that way, no. But that's the way it came across to me. Of course, you don't believe a word of it."

"But I can believe that you do."

"Can you?" Dorothy looked the least bit hopeful. "Can you, Lee? Without thinking me a fool?"

"Oh, I promise you, Mrs. Lowder, I don't think you're a fool!"

And because she thought she was going to weep, she gave her mother-in-law a quick peck on the cheek. But out on the pavement of Central Park West she recovered herself and laughed bitterly at the thought that Mrs. Lowder, as usual, had managed to have the last word.

3

Tony must have heard the telephone several seconds before he awoke. In his dream there had been a battle, a battle that had been somehow glorious. He had been a newcomer to the high command, an officer of strange insignia, possessed of a mystic authority, a visored knight from some dark, exotic kingdom. But his advice had been listened to and his direction followed, and, the day won, the triumphant armies had acclaimed him, raising their shields and shouting. Why had he returned alone at night to the dark and windy battlefield to hear the shrieks of the dying, shrieks that turned the distant cries of victors into squeals over a won parlor game, shrieks that claimed the only reality for themselves and that grew louder and louder until they fused at last into a single deafening roar?

Tony switched on the light by his bed and stared in dazed alarm at the telephone. It seemed a living, threatening thing. Then his thoughts coalesced, and he picked up the receiver. As soon as he had half-whispered "Hello" he heard Lee's voice screeching at him.

"He's blind! Does that satisfy you? He's blind for life. Is that part of your crazy scheme?"

"Lee, *Lee!* Who's blind?"

"Eric, damn you!"

"Lee!"

Eric, poor, earnest, desperate, pedagogic Eric! Eric blind! What kind of madness was she talking? A huge picture of Eric sitting helpless, an open, unseen book in his lap, unrolled in blinding white over his mind. Tony found that he was standing in the middle of the bedroom. Another voice was speaking from the instrument that was still in his hand.

"Tony, this is Pieter Bogardus. Can you hear me? Lee is hysterical. Eric is going to be all right, but he may lose the sight of one eye."

"God! What happened?"

"He was struck on his way to the post office by a hit-and-run driver. He busted his wrist and two ribs and had a concussion. But the eye is the only dangerous thing. The left eye."

"I'll be right there. Where are you?"

"No, Tony, we don't want you. Eric is in a good hospital. He's getting the best of care. You can depend on me to see to that. Your being here would only make Lee worse, and it might increase the boy's danger. Right now he's got maximum police protection."

"Oh, you think . . .?"

"Of course, I think."

"Did anyone see the car?"

"They think it may have been a station wagon with some hippie types that was seen earlier, going very fast. But no doubt the Mafia can choose its mask."

Tony paused and listened to his heart beat in the silence. Then his mind became very clear. He saw that his father-in-law and Lee wanted it to be the Mafia. It helped them to hate him more.

"Is Eric conscious?"

"Just now he's sleeping."

"You've got to let me come."

"Tony, I know what I'm doing. You couldn't find us if you tried, and if you try, the police will pick you up. I give you my word that you will have a detailed report on Eric once a day. The next one will be tomorrow night at eight. Good-bye."

As Tony placed the receiver back in its cradle, the bell instantly rang again. It was Jack Eldon.

"I'm so sorry, Tony. My God, you must be going through hell."

"Do you think it was one of Lassatta's men?"

"I don't, but I suppose we can't be sure."

"You needn't worry. It will make no difference in my testimony."

"Oh, Tony, I didn't mean it that way." There was a pause in which Tony felt that a question was being framed. "Look, Tony, come on around, will you? Judith and I are both up, and we'd love to give you a drink. Don't be alone at a time like this."

To his own surprise, Tony heard himself accept.

As he walked, in a slow, dazed manner, the few blocks to the Eldons' apartment at Park Avenue, he wondered if he would ever be able to come to terms with this new agony. All his mind seemed lit up, like a drab empty auditorium suddenly illuminated at night by the same glaring image of Eric on an infinite screen. But there was nobody in that hall, not even Tony. The web of events that had emerged from the spider's stomach of his bribery had encompassed everybody and nobody. There was nothing as petty as fault. Tony stopped suddenly and moaned aloud in his pain. Something moved beside him, something he had startled. He whirled around and stared into the face of a black youth who had crept up behind him. Tony sprang at him in a sudden passion of excitement, but the man fled away. It was just as well. If ever he could have killed with pleasure, killed with his bare hands, it was then. The mugger had become in a flash the handy symbol of all the evil in the world.

He stood at the deserted corner for several minutes, panting, yearning for another assailant. His clenched fists tingled with the need to make physical contact with an enemy. And then, as nobody came, he recovered himself and walked on.

Judith Eldon was more tactful than he would have thought possible. She made no pretense of not having been to bed, for unlike Jack, who had dressed, she was in her nightgown and robe. She produced hot coffee and drinks and then left the two men alone in the library. Tony gulped down two Scotches without a word and contemplated the near empty decanter.

"There's plenty left where that came from," his host said.

"Oh, two will do me." Looking at Jack's baffled, curious, embarrassed eyes, Tony felt again the impulse of affection. Jack, he thought, was the only friend he had left, the only friend he wanted. The others, all ante-trial, belonged to a lost world. "The last time I was in this room you told me that you couldn't understand my motives. Well, let me tell you something. When Max Leonard confessed, I was about to go to your office to do the same thing. He got in ahead of me and deprived me of all my glory."

Jack jumped up in surprise. "So *that's* the answer! I knew there was something."

"Oh, I was going to be great. I was filled with phony exultation. But life is so damned honest. Just give it a little time and it's sure to puncture your balloon. And so I had to come into court as a nabbed crook. It was better."

"Why, Tony? Why was it better?"

"Because I was better able to face the rottenness in myself when there was no mitigation. It was a wholesome, chastening experience. But it wore off. In a couple of months I was back at my old self-deluding tricks again. Oh, yes, Jack!" Tony threw back his head and laughed bitterly. "When I thought it might have been one of Lassatta's men that had struck at my poor boy's eye, there was a kind of fierce ecstasy in the very agony of it. Like what a martyr feels when the first flames begin to lick at his legs!"

"But you have all the martyr's pain, God knows!" Jack protested. "Don't make it worse for yourself, man."

"I have the pain, yes, but ridiculously. My boy is hurt by some crazy hippies, which has nothing to do with Tony Lowder, who wants to turn the whole universe into his own trial. Oh, I tell you, Jack, there is some crazy plot in the skies to make me humble." Tony got up and went to the mantel and stared at his own wild eyes in the mirror.

"Well, I'm humble enough now, ye powers!" he cried. "I can never be humbler than this."

Jack seemed undecided whether to offer him another drink. Taking in his bewilderment in the mirror Tony turned back to him with a smile. "I'm not crazy, Jack. Don't worry."

"But I don't see why it's so important to be humble," Jack insisted. "You seemed quite humble enough to me from the beginning."

"Ah, but you don't know my heresies. After I rejected God, I had to take over his role. I became my own demiurge, creating my own smaller universe. I had to *be* my mother and *be* my father and *be* my wife. I even had to be my mistress, God help me. I had to suffer their sufferings. I had to live everybody's life but my own. Well, the powers above didn't like that. So they threw a thunderbolt!"

Jack put a consoling hand on his shoulder. "I should say they'd thrown the whole arsenal. But we still have to be in court tomorrow." He glanced at his watch. "Today rather. In exactly six hours. You'd better stay here. I'll give you something that'll make you sleep."

Tony shrugged and followed his host to the guest room. He had reached the point where the only sane thing was to lose consciousness.

4

Joan Conway was lying on her side, huddled up, looking very small in the big canopied royal French bed. She did not move when Lee sat down, as close to her as she could, but their eyes met. Joan's seemed large, for her face was thin and pathetically wasted, but they did not appear to take Lee in. She seemed detached, perhaps even bored.

"I wish I found you better," Lee began conventionally.

"Let's not waste time on that," Joan said in a surprisingly strong voice. "They've given me something, and I'm fine for the moment, but it doesn't last long." She closed her eyes, and after a moment Lee wondered if she had fallen asleep. She looked almost comfortable. Then she opened them. "How's Tony?"

"I haven't seen him."

"That's wrong, you know."

"Don't you think my place has been with Eric?"

"Does Eric think so?"

This was so shrewd a thrust that Lee was taken

aback. She was about to confess that Eric had indeed wanted her to go to Tony when she saw that Joan seemed unconscious again. So she sat and waited and thought of Eric as he had looked that morning, sitting up in the hospital bed that she had brought back to their cottage, one eye concealed under a huge bandage, the other peering bleakly at her. He had become more his old self since the accident, less brooding. But at the same time he seemed resentfully to suspect that she was planning to dedicate her life to becoming his other eye. Eric wanted to get on with the ordinary business of living. He had no time for such exhilarations.

"Will you see Daddy in New York?" he had asked.

"I hadn't planned to. I'm going in to see Mrs. Conway."

Eric had ignored Mrs. Conway. "Don't you think you should?"

"I have some things to work out in myself first."

"You make too much of my eye, Mummie. It wasn't Daddy's fault. And, anyway, they say I'll have partial vision in it. The thing is that we've had enough emotion in this whole business. I've hated Daddy, too. We can't go on hating him forever."

"Eric, there are things about women you can't understand yet. Your father hurt me terribly."

"You mean women don't have to forgive?"

But Lee had not wanted to release her anger. She had not wanted to give up this new occupation of the heart. She had not wanted to share Eric with the man who had let this happen to his son. She had locked the door of herself against Tony and redecorated the interior. It was too early, too trivial, to fling down the bars and cry "all is forgiven!"

She saw now that Joan was looking at her again, and she was ashamed of her preoccupation in the presence of death.

"Why is everyone on Tony's side?" she complained to Joan. "If you heard his mother go on about him, you'd think he was a saint."

"Perhaps he is."

"It's funny you should both think that. I can't imagine two more different women than you and Mrs. Lowder."

"We may have things in common you don't suspect. Desperation, for example. I doubt that Mrs. Lowder ever really believed in anything, not even Tony. I know I didn't."

"Joan, that's absurd! You always believed in all kinds of things: in yourself, in your looks, in your pictures, in your wonderful parties."

"But those were all false gods. Isn't that a classic truth? They fell to bits the moment I got cancer. That was the time when Mother Lowder and I became spiritual twins. When we were down. Bereft. Shorn. It's easier for people like us to be converted than people like you."

"People like *me!*" Lee exclaimed in surprise. "What kind of people are people like me?"

"People who still have false gods."

"And what are mine?"

"Tony. Or your ideal of Tony. Or love." Joan pronounced the word with a mocking emphasis that must have tired her, for she closed her eyes again. Lee, again waiting, found herself struck by the implications of Joan's idea. For who had encouraged her resentment of Tony's behavior more than her father and who had more false gods than he? When she thought of the mantelpiece of his mind, it seemed crowded to the choking point with little waxen lares and penates.

"Do you want me to go?" she whispered at last.

Joan appeared to smile. "Not yet."

"Oh, Joan, isn't it terrible?" Lee exclaimed in sudden shame. "Here I should be consoling you, and I'm the one who's asking for help!"

"Why not? *I* don't have to do anything."

"You're really reconciled to dying?" When Lee had spoken, she could hardly believe that she had been so crude, but Joan's eyes showed no resentment. She was obviously beyond any power that Lee might have to create doubt or confusion. Her voice took on a note of amused speculation.

"I'm like poor Lucy in that poem of Wordsworth's," she murmured, her eyes still closed. "I'm rolling round and round, with rocks and stones and trees."

"I see. It's wonderful!" Lee had lost the last shred of the superiority of the living. "But how has Tony helped you?"

Joan opened her eyes and looked at Lee with more focus now. "It was that Sunday. When you came to Long Island. Tony convinced me that he was unhappier than I was."

"And that did it?"

"Well, don't you see, if he was unhappier than *I* was, he had to be in hell. And if there was a hell, didn't there have to be a heaven?"

"For you, you mean?"

"Oh, and for Tony, too. He wouldn't have to stay in hell. It was the sign I'd been looking for. Like that chalice in the Cloisters. A sign that something else existed."

"And that was enough?"

Again there was a trace of a smile on Joan's lips. "It was enough for me. I've grown humble."

This time she seemed really to go to sleep. Lee rose and stood at the end of the bed.

"You *are* humble," she half-whispered. "I think I envy you."

"You needn't." Lee heard what she thought was almost a chuckle from the bed. "There's nothing that's going to happen to me that isn't going to happen to you."

Was it really a new, a redeemed Joan Conway talking? Or was it the old Joan Conway, with a greater ego than ever, the Joan Conway who had to have everything better than anyone else's, who would help herself, like a barbaric czarina, to as many slices of Lee's husband as she wished? The Joan who now demanded heaven as her birthright? But Lee was not to find out, for the trained nurse came in now and indicated with a severe little smile and a sharp nod that the visit was over.

5

On the last day of the defense's case in *United States* v. *Lassatta et al.* Max watched Tony's final appearance in the witness chair. It varied little from his others. He was patient, courteous, relentless in his consistency. Lanigan's small bag of tricks was emptied, refilled and emptied again before this unmovable witness. But Max's reaction was now different from what it had been. He was not bitter or angry or even afraid.

He had been careful to avoid Tony. Even in court recesses he had turned away from the latter's friendly smiles. If betrayal were a laughing matter to Tony, it was not so to him. Both he and Tony had betrayed and been betrayed, and he was not so superficial or so macabre as to want to pick the white bones of friendship out of the ashes of *that* grate. And now he had awakened to the sudden discovery that love and hate seemed all at once to have expired and that he could watch Tony testify without the least apparent emotion. The man in the witness chair struck him as simply futile. Was *that* the secret of the great Tony? That he was a bit of an ass?

The day was bitterly cold outside, but the heat in the courtroom was high, and Max, who loved to be warm, stirred luxuriously under his sweater and jacket. He felt a torpor spreading through his limbs and body that made him think of his conscious spirit as detached from the flesh, as if he were a kind of Ariel watching, unseen, the watchers in that terrible courtroom. The idea of his future, which up until then had been little better than a nightmare, seemed almost agreeable, almost pleasantly exciting. It had been arranged that he should work in a liquor store in Panama City under the name of Howard Lamb. He would have an apartment only a block from where he worked, near a beach. Max knew a little Spanish, and he now had a vision of a life of sunbathing in a town of white stucco and red roofs by a sapphire sea. All right, suppose this *were* euphoric. What was wrong with euphoria? Particularly in his case. Might not Panama be a heaven attained without dying, a paradise with all the desperate pressures of his old life removed? He would not even be able to contemplate making a success of business there, for success would destroy the anonymity that was the very point of his new life. Howard Lamb would not have to be anything. He would not even have to be a man. He could pick up his harp and wander, caroling, through the golden streets of the new Jerusalem!

And he could make new friends. Max's mind raced ahead now. He could have love affairs. He could implement all his dirtiest thoughts. He could lie on a beach, naked in the mild breeze, with his arm around the neck of a dark Panamanian boy. He could . . .

There was a rustle of rising about him as the court recessed. Max jumped up with sudden energy and strode out to the corridor to smoke. Then he started in fear as somebody touched his elbow, but he relaxed when he saw it was a woman. It took him several seconds to realize that it was Lee Lowder.

"What's wrong, Max? Don't you know me?"

He continued to stare at her. Her face was oddly expressionless. "I didn't think you'd still speak to me."

Lee's blank gaze conveyed her indifference. "After all that's happened to us, there can't be any more enemies."

"Only survivors?"

"Have we survived?"

"I heard you were going to divorce Tony."

"Wouldn't it be wise?"

"Oh, when a ship is sinking . . ." He shrugged.

"One shouldn't mind being called a rat?" she finished for him.

"Why should you be called any name but the one you pick? I'm going to take a new one."

She nodded. "I see. You can do that. And Joan can die. And I can become Mrs. Bogardus. So there'll be nobody left but Tony."

"He asked for it. His whole life has been a bungle. Going from one hack to another in quest of his soul. When did he think of us?"

"How you say that! As if you were some god sneering down at a poor fool of a human being."

"I don't sneer at Tony. I don't even pity him. I

see him. That's all. He made the wrong choice. He made the wrong choice and destroyed us all."

"Did he destroy himself?"

"Ah, I was waiting for that!" Max cried with sudden bitterness. "The final argument of Tony's woman! That Tony, for all his faults, for all his blundering, has still that spark of life that is worth all our carcasses! You'll go back to him, Lee. Mark my words. You'll go back to him."

"And that will be such a mistake?"

"Oh, Lee." Max threw up his hands. "You and Tony and your consciences. Look what you've brought me to. And you never even really liked me, either of you. You both resented my trying to make Tony a great man. Tony didn't want to be one, and you wanted him to owe it all to you."

"Ah, I have you now!" Lee exclaimed. "You're not a god, after all. Your Olympian detachment is a phony. You hate us, Max. Admit it!"

"Hate you and Tony?"

"No. You hate us women!"

Max turned away from her, quivering in disgust. "I rather think I do," he muttered. As he walked into the courtroom and caught Lassatta's eye, instantly averted, all his panic returned. Even Panama did not seem so far away now. He thought he was going to burst into tears. Damn Lee!

6

Tony sat in the courtroom on a bench by himself waiting for Judge Fenton to enter. The talking voices around him seemed to come from outside the imagined shell of immunity that encased him. He had seen Lee, looking very small and still in the back of the room. They had nodded, but he had not spoken to her. Eldon's secretary had told him that she wanted to wait till after the sentencing when the guard would take him back to the office.

The rustle around him of rising people and the distant drone of the clerk announced the arrival of the Judge.

"In *United States* against *Lassatta, Menzies et al.*, I shall proceed to sentencing. Will the defendant Anthony Lowder step forward?"

Tony approached the bench. The Judge's friendly brown face, the face of the fellow lawyer, the fellow committeeman—for he and Tony had once served on the same committee of the City Bar

Association—the face of a paradise excluding Lucifer, of a warm, happy nursery closing its door to a forlorn but wicked child, grew long and stern and detached. Yet the voice was not hostile. It was merely dry.

"I have done much thinking on your case, Lowder. It has been a most distressing one at the bar. That you, an attorney of good reputation, a candidate for high public office and the holder of a sensitive government post, should take a bribe to betray your trust is a sorry fact that will feed the venom of those who claim today that our whole system is rotten to the core. On the other hand, I take into consideration your openness and candor in this trial and your complete cooperation with the prosecution. Because of the negative nature of your crime I have been led to believe that a conviction of the defendants would have been vastly more difficult without this cooperation. I sentence you to one year in a federal penitentiary."

Tony stepped back and started to follow the guard from the chamber. The Judge was already proceeding to his next calendar item. As Tony passed Lassatta the latter reached out and caught his arm. Tony leaned down.

"I am sorry about your kid."

Tony returned his stare. "Are you?"

"You think I had anything to do with it? Forget it. We're not that sort."

"But there are things you do that are just as bad."

Lassatta's face became inscrutable. "Look, Lowder, I just wanted to say I was sorry about your kid."

"I don't want your sympathy."

Lassatta's whisper became almost inaudible. "You could do with it, you know."

Tony shrugged and straightened up. "You don't understand. I'm beyond all that. *Way* beyond."

In Jack's office, after the guard had closed the door, Tony and Lee looked at each other for several moments. His first reflection was that she must have lost five pounds. Certainly, she looked that many years older.

"Your hair hasn't gone gray," he observed. "I'm surprised."

"I haven't dyed it, either."

"It was good of you to come to my sentencing. I assume it wasn't to gloat."

"Eric wanted me to."

"How is Eric?"

"He's making out. He wants to go back to school."

"And Isabel?"

"She's gone back. She's staying with Mother and Daddy. Do you think it's safe?"

"I think it's the only way. I think life's going to be hard enough without their running scared."

"I agree."

He knew that there had to be resentment behind such impassivity, but he decided it would be better to leave it until she chose to bring it out.

"Have you decided what you're going to do?" she asked. "After you get out? Mr. Eldon thinks it may be soon."

"Can I come home?"

"You mean to the apartment?"

"Where else?"

"To me and the children?" Her tone seemed startled.

"Where else?"

She was silent for a moment. "Yes, if you want."

"Would *you* want?"

"I don't think that matters." Her brown eyes were leaden. "What matters is the children. And I think, all things considered, it might be better if you did come back."

"Good. We're agreed on that, too."

"But what will you do? For a job, I mean. I'm told you can't practice law."

"Jack Eldon has offered me a position in his family's company. They sell office equipment. I'd be a salesman. On the road most of the time. Buffalo, Syracuse, Albany. I guess I'd better take it."

"He certainly takes care of his witnesses."

"He takes care of this one. Jack's become a real friend. I guess that's something I'm going to need."

"Oh, you." She shrugged. "You and your charm. You'll get by."

He ignored this. "It was the travel side of the job that attracted me. I thought my being away part of the time might lessen the strain at home. Having Daddy back is going to be a bit embarrassing at first."

"I see you have it all figured out."

"I've had time."

"But can you face the future with any *hope,* Tony?" she asked, with something like exasperation now in her tone. "Can you face it with any enthusiasm?"

"Yes. Because I'll have a job to do."

"You'll like being a salesman?"

"I might, but I didn't mean that. I meant the big job. The job of trying to save Eric from bitterness. And Isabel from self-pity. And you." He paused and then gave her a fixed, deliberate smile. "And you," he repeated softly. "From despair."

The small yellow spark in her irises might have been curiosity. "It's quite a challenge, isn't it? Perhaps you'll even enjoy it."

"I'll try to. I'll need every weapon I've got."

"What a commentary on life!" Lee walked to the window, as if propelled by a sudden surge of impatience. "That the only way to give it any meaning is to make a mess so you can clean it up." Her voice shook now as she seemed to address an imagined audience. "Are you bored with life? Do you find it ugly and futile? No problem. Get a heaping garbage can, trundle it into your front parlor and kick it over. Then you'll have a job that will save your soul. Surely there must be a God to have thought up a system like that."

"I know it sounds ridiculous. But in my plight I must put up with the ridiculous."

"And what about me?" she cried at last in passion, turning back to him. "What do we do about *me?* What if I can't learn to love you again?"

"That, I'm afraid, is your problem."

"Do you love me?"

"Certainly."

"I don't believe it!"

"Don't, then." He realized all at once how exhausted he was. The strain of the sentencing had been greater than he had been aware, and Lee's emotional persistence was trying. "I can't be always interfering between you and your rationalizations. That was one of the things wrong with the old Tony. Interfering between people and their favorite punishments."

"Joan's dead, you know."

"Yes. I'm glad it's over."

"Do you think her cancer was a favorite punishment?"

"Who knows?"

"Oh, don't be so damn above it all!" Lee stamped on the floor. "You don't care about Joan *or* about me. You look placidly down from the peak of your great self-knowledge."

"I'm tired, Lee."

"So am I! Tell me just one thing, and I'll go. Do you really think God spoke to you that Sunday at Joan's? Do you really believe he leaned down from heaven to communicate personally with Tony Lowder?"

He watched her in silence until some of the petulance had drained out of her expression. "I've thought a lot about it, but I haven't any real clue. It seemed to come from outside of me."

"*Seemed.*"

"Well, of course, seemed. I can't know, can I? But I don't think it was only the product of my psyche, if that's what you're getting at. I think that I was somehow in tune—or out of tune—with chords that were not in *me*. And that's all. That's really all. It was a purely negative experience. It has not been repeated. There has been no corresponding visitation urging me to do anything or believe in anything. All I know is that I took a bribe and went to hell. But that has to be enough to build a life on."

"Will it be?"

"*I* think it will be."

Lee suddenly sobbed. "I don't know what to think of you!"

"Try to love me."

"But you're a monster!"

"Try to love a monster, then."

"*Can* one?"

"Please, Lee. I suddenly feel absolutely pooped. I guess I can't take any more of this. Later on, maybe. Why don't you go now?"

But she sat down at Jack's desk and covered her face. "Just tell me this," she begged. "If I *do* learn to love you again, will there be only me? No Joans, I mean?"

He closed his eyes. The exhaustion was complete. "You didn't mind Joan that much. Your trouble is that you're jealous of God."

"Oh, Tony! Don't be so . . . horrible!"

"But you are. You must take consolation in the fact that he may not exist. Or that I may not believe in him. Don't worry. I may not."

She got to her feet, cold, rebuffed. "Shall I see you before you go to the penitentiary? Mr. Eldon says I may."

"Of course."

"When?"

"Tomorrow, if you want."

"Tony, *help* me!" she cried.

"I will, darling. Tomorrow."

She turned at this and almost ran from the room. Tony sighed in relief. Now he could sit down, as he yearned to do. But the moment he was seated, he seemed to revive. He looked about Jack's bare chamber and thought of his own apartment and the living room in the evening. He saw Eric with a black patch over his eye, working on a problem in an algebra book. He saw Isabel, stouter, chewing gum, listening to a radio crooner. He saw Lee doing nothing. Just sitting there, moody, disconsolate, waiting for him. What else could she be waiting for? What else could any of them be waiting for? And the realization that they might not have to wait in vain filled him suddenly with a happiness that made him jump up and cry aloud. Happy? Surely Lee was right. He *was* a monster. But monsters could still be men.